"I have a meeting tonight," he told her, walking her to his office door. "But I'd like to take you out to dinner tomorrow."

Tomorrow, all his plans would start to stitch together.

He smiled at her in the way that usually had her softening. And it was intoxicating to make this woman soften. She was young enough he'd thought she'd be naive. Biddable.

Saverina was none of those things, but luckily she'd taken to him anyway. And tomorrow, she would agree to be his bride.

Saverina was a tool, a means to an end, but one he was prepared to lie to for the rest of his life, if necessary.

When she smiled up at him, a silent agreement to be waiting for him, he knew that he would succeed.

Thrive, he told himself. Because what was better success and satisfaction than revenge against the man who'd made his mother's life hell?

Teo would pay any price to win that game.

Lorraine Hall is a part-time hermit and full-time writer. She was born with an old soul and her head in the clouds, which, it turns out, is the perfect combination to spend her days creating thunderous alpha heroes and the fierce, determined heroines who win their hearts. She lives in a potentially haunted house with her soulmate and rambunctious band of hermits-in-training. When she's not writing romance, she's reading it.

Books by Lorraine Hall

Harlequin Presents

The Prince's Royal Wedding Demand
A Son Hidden from the Sicilian
The Forbidden Princess He Craves

Secrets of the Kalyva Crown

Hired for His Royal Revenge
Pregnant at the Palace Altar

Visit the Author Profile page at Harlequin.com.

Lorraine Hall

PLAYING THE SICILIAN'S
GAME OF REVENGE

HARLEQUIN
PRESENTS

HARLEQUIN®
PRESENTS™

Recycling programs
for this product may
not exist in your area.

ISBN-13: 978-1-335-59325-2

Playing the Sicilian's Game of Revenge

Copyright © 2024 by Lorraine Hall

For questions and comments about the quality of this book,
please contact us at CustomerService@Harlequin.com.

Harlequin Enterprises ULC
22 Adelaide St. West, 41st Floor
Toronto, Ontario M5H 4E3, Canada
www.Harlequin.com

Printed in U.S.A.

PLAYING THE SICILIAN'S
GAME OF REVENGE

CHAPTER ONE

SAVERINA PARISI HAD spent the past year proving her brother wrong. She loved her oldest brother, but that didn't mean she didn't celebrate this victory.

When she was fresh out of university, *he* had thought she should take a gap year. Spend time thinking about what she really wanted to do with her life. The only thing Saverina had wanted to do was belong in her billionaire brother's company.

She had made him a deal. She would be his assistant, where he could keep an eye on her, for six months. If she did a good job and still wanted to work at Parisi, she could stay. If she hated it, or was terrible at it, she would have to go take that gap year.

Maybe she should have taken the gap year as so many people weren't afforded that luxury, she knew, but all she could think was at this age her brother had been building empires—all to save the family. She wanted to be part of the material thing that *had* saved them from the awful poverty they'd grown up in. She wanted to help Lorenzo in some way that might be a *little* repayment for all he'd given her.

So for six months she had been an *excellent* assistant. Never afraid to take an angry phone call, to soothe ruffled feathers, to tell someone to wait. She had no problem working her way up in her brother's company, any more than she had a problem with people whispering about how she got the job.

The Parisis had come from nothing, so she had no qualms about using all her brother's considerable wealth and influence to do what needed doing. She owed it to Lorenzo and all he'd sacrificed for the family. She owed it to the sister they'd lost who'd never had a chance to succeed.

But mostly, she owed it to herself.

When her six months were up, even exacting Lorenzo couldn't find fault with her effort. She was allowed to stay on. She would remain as Lorenzo's assistant until the end of the year, then decide what direction she wanted to go in within Parisi Enterprises.

She'd planned to dive into the different sides of the business and decide where she wanted to put her talents to use. IT would have been the best fit for the skills she'd learned and honed at university, but it also had a lot of room for error.

Saverina Parisi didn't do error.

Instead, she'd been distracted. And now Teo LaRosa was much more than a distraction. The handsome executive currently zooming up the ranks with no connections whatsoever had gone from an ill-advised date to a full-fledged relationship in the course of a few whirlwind months, even if they were still keeping it a secret.

Which was why she was purposefully ignoring the fluttering butterflies in her stomach and the way her pulse seemed to *pound* in her neck while she waited for Teo to give his assistant the go-ahead for her to be let into his office.

She needed to speak to him briefly for work. Her brother was on an extended holiday with his growing family, so Saverina's duties took her to Teo's office often. Each and every time, they behaved perfectly professionally...

But all the man needed to do was smile at her to have her knees going a little weak.

It was strange to be this woman. When she had flicked *boys* off at the slightest irritation all through university. She had *never* felt out of control of her own heart, let alone impulses.

Only Teo twisted her into a million knots she didn't understand.

Saverina considered herself incredibly world-wise. She'd lost her mother and sister under tragic circumstances and had been nothing but relieved when her father had drunk himself to death. All before she'd hit her teens. Since then, she'd been raised by a workaholic brother. She thought she knew just about everything—or certainly enough—until Teo had kissed her.

Now the world was different, and she wasn't quite so sure of her place in it. But she knew without a shadow of a doubt that she wanted to be next to Teo.

"Ms. Parisi, Mr. LaRosa will see you now," Teo's stiff, stern assistant offered. Mrs. Caruso had been working for Parisi since its inception. Saverina had watched her be nothing but warm and kind to Teo, to Lorenzo, and a cold wall of ice to literally everyone else.

So she didn't take the woman's cool gaze—all the way through the door—as an offense. Mrs. Caruso was doing her job and wasn't easily swayed by the Parisi last name.

Saverina much preferred that to the type of people who sidled up to her or sucked up to her simply because of her connection to Lorenzo. Besides, she'd learned how to live under scrutiny in a million different ways as the sister to a self-made billionaire, especially when his supposed bad deeds had been splashed across gossip sites years before.

Inside Teo's large office, new in the past month thanks to all his hard work, the man in question sat at his desk, head slightly bowed as he finished typing something on his phone.

His dark hair was swept back, ruthlessly styled always—well, except after hours when she got her hands on it. His shoulders were broad, something that was evident even with him sitting down behind his desk. He glanced up, his dark eyes still half-distracted by whatever had been on his phone.

His face could have been sculpted out of marble. High, sharp cheekbones, an aristocratic nose. All edges and angles except for the sensual promise of his lips. She loved the way that mouth felt against her skin.

She kept waiting for that breathless, foolish feeling to go away in his presence, but it never did. And every time it didn't, it caused her daydreams to get more out of hand. Trusting him enough to let him into her bed—well, *his* bed, since she still lived at Lorenzo's estate—had been one thing, but now she was thinking toward things like *love* and *forever*.

She despaired of herself. But when he smiled at her and got to his feet, all despair was replaced with a warmth and longing so tangled and deep it threatened to make her forget *everything*, when she was a woman who always had her wits about her.

Or had been. Before him.

She cleared her throat and moved forward, taking the seat opposite him at his desk. She looked up at him, fixed her most businesslike expression on her face, and tapped the notebook she'd brought. "Lorenzo has extended his vacation, so we'll have to discuss moving some of next week's meetings further out."

Teo stood there, staring down at her for a moment, before he said anything. A moment when she felt his eyes take a tour of her body—as she'd hoped.

She had dressed knowing she would have a meeting with him today, opting for a skirt over pants and a blouse the color of strawberries that skimmed her figure rather than hid it.

It was all very professional, but it definitely wasn't sexless.

"You have access to my calendar, do you not?" he finally said, that dark, delicious voice of his threatening to turn her insides to absolute *mush*. "You couldn't have just changed the meetings?"

"No," she replied, feigning—perhaps a little exaggeratedly—shock and disdain. "Not everyone is prudent about filling out their schedules, and you know how Lorenzo is about changing things. We need to make certain no more reschedules happen." Which was, of course, ridiculous, because Lorenzo was the one rescheduling in the first place.

But she liked having an excuse to see Teo at work, and it *was* often easier to meet face-to-face to make schedule changes rather than trade endless back-and-forth emails. Or so she told herself.

"We must behave ourselves at work, Saverina," he said, and she supposed he meant it to sound scolding, but the curve of his mouth and the heat in his eyes undermined his words.

"I don't recall suggesting otherwise," she responded brightly. This man had turned her world upside down, sure, but she was still *herself*. Inwardly she might quake a little, but even when Teo got under her skin, under her defenses, she didn't let *him* know that.

She hoped.

Teo LaRosa was not a good man. He knew this every time he put his hands on Saverina Parisi and did not tell her the truth. Every time he watched with too much interest as she crossed her legs in his office.

As he did now. She was a beautiful woman. Smart,

and so quick-witted it nearly knocked him off his axis on a daily basis. Even if he had not targeted her, he might have found himself interested in her.

But he had targeted her. From the start. After this job, she was the key to his plan for revenge. Retribution would always be more important than goodness or truth.

No matter the surprise of Saverina Parisi.

"I believe your *eyes* were suggesting otherwise, *bedda*," he said, enjoying these interludes when they were just alone enough to flirt, arouse, seduce…but at work and unable to go through with any of it. Until tonight.

After.

It had been no hardship wooing her. She was beautiful. Clever. He hadn't even really *planned* to take her to bed. It had just sort of…happened. The chemistry was undeniable.

It was hard, sometimes, to remember that she was a means to an end over someone to be enjoyed. But at the end of the day, he always remembered.

Just as he always remembered what Dante Marino had said to him the first and last time Teo had approached him.

I will crush you if you try.

Teo would never be crushed. He would use everything in his power—this job with Dante's worst enemy, a soon-to-be engagement to said worst enemy's sister—to not just flourish, but to crush Dante first. In every way that would hurt the man's substantial pride and reputation.

Saverina was a tool, but this would not hurt her in any real way. Her beloved brother also hated Dante Marino. So Teo did not consider this *using* her, exactly. They enjoyed each other. And when she married him, he would be a suitable husband. He would provide for her in the lifestyle to which she was accustomed. He would be kind—or his version of kind. He would never drag her name through the mud or embarrass her, and he would certainly never treat her in a way that would make her fear for her life.

That was a Dante Marino specialty, and Teo had promised himself the moment he'd discovered the truth that he would never be anything like his biological father.

Perhaps he could not love Saverina as such a young, beautiful woman deserved to be loved. He had no use for love, for children, for families…all those delicate things that could be lost. But he would give her a good life.

She would never need know that she was a tool or a pawn.

They rearranged the necessary schedules, and Teo fixed them into his computerized calendar himself while simultaneously noting them down in his paper planner as that always helped him remember things without having to look at them again.

He had not risen in the ranks at Parisi Enterprises by being careless or relying on anyone else, even an assistant, though he had one at his disposal now. He had worked hard, kept all his cards close to the vest, and given Saverina space and time to arrive in his orbit rather than go after her so obviously.

Teo knew how to be patient. He knew how to lay a trap. But most of all, Teo LaRosa knew how to survive.

Now he was on the precipice of *thriving*. As he'd promised his mother he would after she'd made those world-altering deathbed confessions.

He had the unwanted image of his mother, small and frail and wasting away in a hospital bed, lodged in his mind, and needed to erase it. The way he'd been doing for the past two years.

Focus on his revenge.

"That should be all," Saverina said, rising from her seat. He rose too, enjoying the way she didn't quite meet his gaze. He knew if she did, her cheeks would go pink, and she didn't want to leave his office flushed and flustered.

It filled him with an emotion he could not quite identify that he could do both to her.

"I have a meeting tonight," he told her, walking her to his office door. "But I'd like to take you out to dinner tomorrow." Usually he gave her more details, but tomorrow would be special. Tomorrow, all his plans would start to stitch together.

She would say yes to his proposal. He had no doubt. But he also saw the little flash of suspicion in her eyes at this moment. Since she had privy to his schedule and knew the meeting wasn't business, she was suspicious. She likely thought it something as mundane as seeing another woman behind her back.

Teo was not mundane.

He smiled at her in the way that usually had her softening. And it was intoxicating to make this woman soften. She was young enough he'd thought she'd be naive. Biddable.

Saverina was none of those things, but luckily she'd taken to him anyway. And tomorrow, she would agree to be his bride.

But tonight, he had some things to set in motion.

"The meeting is with the lawyer of my mother's estate," he explained, even though the explanation was a lie. "It shouldn't take all evening. If you'd like, you can let yourself into my place, and I'll text you when I'm on my way."

His mother had no estate. There were no lawyers. There were only the men he'd hired to get the DNA from Dante required to then test it against his.

Proof was the first step.

Destruction was the second.

Saverina was a tool, a means to an end, but one he was prepared to lie to for the rest of his life, if necessary.

When she smiled up at him, a silent agreement to be waiting for him, he knew that he would succeed.

Thrive, he told himself. Because what was better success and satisfaction than revenge against the man who'd made his mother's life hell?

Teo would pay any price to win that game.

CHAPTER TWO

SAVERINA WALKED INTO Teo's luxury apartment after being let into the building by the doorman, who knew her by sight now. Since she lived with Lorenzo and his family—because she loved spending time with her niece and nephew, and because Lorenzo's estate was big enough that she could *feel* like she lived on her own if she wanted to—Teo had never met her there.

Maybe she should broach going public with him. She'd been just as keen to keep their relationship a secret at first—both because of their positions at Parisi and because…well, she'd wanted to make sure this was something…real first. Deep down, she knew it was a little silly, but she couldn't stand the thought of *failing* in her brother's and sister-in-law's eyes.

And maybe, in the dark of Teo's lavish apartment, she could admit to herself it wasn't just failing in front of Lorenzo. It was failing…*period*. She didn't think anyone—even her brothers and sisters—knew just how hard she worked to make her entire life look like effortless success.

She felt as if she owed them that. After all they'd sacrificed, so much more terrible things they'd seen during their traumatic childhood, and the loss of her eldest sister—Saverina wanted them all to believe her life was *easy* and everything she wanted. She hoped they thought her spoiled and frivolous and successful. Without a care in the world.

She blew out a breath, frustrated at the serious tone of her thoughts today. Ever since that meeting with Teo this afternoon, she'd been out of sorts. He'd never mentioned this "meeting" of his until today, and she didn't know why it had felt...off.

It wasn't right to be suspicious. He'd given her no reason to be, and he had every right to be a little... strange regarding a meeting with his late mother's estate lawyer. She knew he had no father in the picture, and his mother's death had been a long, drawn-out affair—though he'd never been specific about what illness had taken her life.

Saverina hadn't pressed because she knew not just the pain of losing a mother long before you were ready, but the way the circumstances behind it could twist inside of you. The way it felt better to hold it in some dark place inside rather than discuss it ad nauseam.

Besides, if he was really off doing something that would damage their relationship, would he have invited her to be here tonight? She liked to think *no*. But a little voice inside of her that had never trusted a man outside her family before whispered *maybe*.

Frustrated with herself, she didn't bother with the

lights. She walked through the apartment and out to her favorite part of it. The curving balcony that looked out over the city. In the daylight, you could see the Madonie Mountains stretch out beyond the ancient spires and sleek lines of Palermo's architecture. At night, the city sparkled until it all went dark past the beach and in the midst of the Gulf of Palermo.

Saverina stepped into the cool evening and breathed in deep. She'd long planned to spend her life alone. Happily single. Like Lorenzo. But then he'd gone and gotten himself married and built a family. And if *Lorenzo* could believe in something like love, then surely it existed. Surely it could exist for her too.

No one had warned her it would be *terrifying*. No one had explained to her that she might have a riot of feelings inside her she didn't know how to put to words. And worse, that she might not have any idea how the person on the receiving end felt about all this emotion.

Sex was easy, she'd found, and suddenly in retrospect understood a lot of her classmates better. Love, on the other hand, was complicated.

Did she love Teo? She was almost certain she did. Did he love her? She thought he *acted* as though he did, but he never gave her the words.

Should she tell him first? Part of her knew she should. Silly and old-fashioned—something she refused to be—to wait for him to say it first.

But she supposed that fear of looking like a failure, like something might be *effort*, like she was putting something on the line…well, it wasn't just about her siblings. The idea of telling Teo she loved him to be met with anything other than fall-to-his-knees gratitude left her feeling sick to her stomach.

Luckily she didn't have to dwell on those conflicting thoughts any longer, because she heard the apartment door open. Forcefully. He stepped inside, the anger vibrating off of him.

Until he saw her. He stilled. It was only the flash of a second, that fury in his eyes, but the daughter of an alcoholic father and drug-addicted mother knew how to look for flashes. How to brace for the storms that might come in the aftermath.

She entered the room carefully, aware of every inch of her body. It wasn't that she was afraid of him like she'd been afraid of her father. Teo had never been anything remotely close to violent. But temper and words could hurt, and though he'd never unleashed those on her, she knew the potential existed.

"Is everything okay?" she asked, keeping her voice carefully neutral.

He stared at her for a moment in complete silence, and she watched him put it all away. With a breath and some internal control, all those storms calmed into peace.

She found she didn't believe that peace, even when she wanted to. All she could do was want to help him find the real thing.

The meeting had not gone well, and it delayed his many plans and put Teo in a foul mood. So foul he'd forgotten he'd told Saverina to be here in the first place. He'd forgotten about her entirely, so he was not at all prepared to deal with her as he usually was.

This was what came of being too confident. He'd gotten cocky and made a few missteps this evening. Now he had to deal with the consequences. He knew better, and that twisted his self-directed anger more than the rest.

He hid his fisted hand in a pocket. The role he played for Saverina was not an angry man, not a man with a temper. But it boiled inside of him tonight, and he did not know how to tame it.

Because they had not gotten the necessary DNA. The men he'd hired said it could be another week before they had a chance. A *week*. Now he didn't know if he should postpone the engagement or go forward with it. He didn't know whether to hire new men or stick with the ones who'd promised him careful, clandestine results.

He didn't *know*, and it left him wanting to *rage*. He had to get rid of her without raising any suspicions or concerns, because he did not wish his anger to concern Saverina. And he needed quiet solitude to reconfigure his upended plans.

"Teo?" Saverina said, a little hesitantly. She didn't act *afraid*, but he saw her concern and endeavored to beat back everything roiling inside of him.

"Everything is fine," he said, but his voice was not convincing. Even he knew it sounded hard-edged and mean. "I thought this would be my last meeting with the lawyer, but he informed me we are not quite done yet. I was eager for it to be…over." He didn't see the problem with a little truth mixed in with the lies. That's how he'd won her over, after all. "It's put me in a foul temper."

She let out a little sound, like a sigh, then fully crossed the room to him. "It must be very hard," she murmured, reaching out to him. Ready to soothe.

She did not. If anything, she did the opposite. She was merely a pawn, but she was here in his space, offering kindness, and he did not deserve it. He could not *take* it.

He grabbed her hands before she could wrap her arms around him, stopping her in her tracks. "I will have to apologize and excuse myself. I'm in a terrible mood, and I cannot see putting it to rights tonight. Perhaps you should just go home." He'd tacked on the *perhaps* because if there was anything he fully understood about Saverina, even in this mood, it was that she did not respond well to *demands*.

"Perhaps," she agreed easily, but she just stood there, his hand enclosing her slim wrists. She did not attempt to pull away or push forward. She simply stood there, a bit like a prisoner.

It clawed at him, along with the sympathy he saw in her eyes. Not pity. Just warmth and kindness and everything she should not give him. Did she have no sense of self-preservation?

"But perhaps," she continued softly, "I should stay, as I am not only here to enjoy your good moods and happiness."

For a moment, he had no words. He could not move at all. He had careful lines, and they all led to *revenge*. Not complications. He had already blurred too many personal lines with her—having her in his bed, discussing his mother's death no matter how superficially, and if he did not get rid of her *now*, he would no doubt cross yet more lines.

Disastrous.

But insisting she leave, drawing that hard line, would also be a problem. She would not care for it, and if he was to go through with his proposal plans, he could not afford to make her angry or upset. If he lost her now...

No. He would not fail this. Perhaps he had to alter his other plans, but he would not alter the ones that made him a Parisi by marriage. *That* would hurt Dante as much as anything else. So *that* was what Teo lived for.

He forced himself to release her, to breathe. He could not will the storms away, but he could steer the ship through them. "I'll just get myself a drink. Would you like something?"

He started to move for his kitchen, but she stopped him, her palm sliding up his chest as she hooked her other arm around his neck.

"How about this instead." She lifted to her toes and pressed her mouth to his. It was sweet, but he only felt fire. A dangerous mix of frustration and want. The offer of something he wanted, after the denial of what he needed.

It made the kiss dangerous. Untethered. So often the chemistry between them surprised him into going further than he'd planned with her, wanting more than he should from her. But this was different, because the lack of control was both about her and what had happened earlier tonight.

He wasn't at his best. He wasn't thinking straight. He could not control that careful line he walked. So the kiss became wild. He held her too tightly, dove into the taste of her too deeply, lost in everything she offered. He had never allowed himself such an utter lack of walls built against his needs.

This would threaten everything.

Still, he couldn't gentle the kiss, his grip on her. Everything in him resisted the knowledge he needed to pull away. Set her back. Wait until he could control himself. Take this step by step. Slake his lust, and hers, knowing he was in control.

Control. Always control.

Finally he managed to wrench his mouth from hers, their breaths mingling in harsh gasps for air. Her mouth swollen, her eyes heavy-lidded and needy. It took every last ounce of willpower to resist.

He had to resist. Didn't he?

"If I take you to bed tonight, Saverina, I do not have it within myself to be gentle," he growled. The best warning he could muster as needs and wants and thwarted desires jangled in his gut like a dangerous concoction set to explode.

Her dark eyes studied him for a long moment before she spoke—not pulling away in the slightest. "Who said you had to be?" She nipped at his lip, teeth scraping just enough to cause a quick, sharp stab of pain underneath a potent arrow of pleasure.

"I'm not made of glass," she continued. "I'm certainly not fragile. Is that what you think of me?"

He had no answer for that shocking response, no reason over the roar of his blood, the tightness in his body that she'd put there. He tried to hold on to all his control, all his plans, everything he was.

"Be honest with me, Teo. If that's rough, so be it." Then she pulled his mouth down to hers once more and...if this was what she wanted, if this was all her doing, he wasn't losing his control. Ruining his plans.

He was only enjoying what she offered. He could not give her honesty in all things, but he could give her the honesty of how he wanted her in this moment—because she wanted it too.

So he didn't bother with the buttons of her blouse, simply tore as he ravaged her mouth with his. He tried to pull the shirt off of her, but it got caught there, trapping her arms behind her back, stuck in the sleeves of her shirt.

He pressed her against the wall, needing something he could not articulate, could not find. He pulled back from her mouth, but there was no anxiety in her gaze, no tightness in her shoulders. She didn't shake her head or warn him off. She met his gaze, direct, intense.

"Well, don't stop," she murmured.

So perfect, boldness and fire at odds with the delicate form of her. He kissed her once more, her mouth, her cheek, her neck. Then went ahead and used his teeth, scraped down the slim, elegant curve of her neck. Her sigh was a shudder as he jerked her skirt up.

Need was a molten river. There was no finesse. Just a race to be one. To chase all of these tangles inside of them to some precipice that felt, in the moment, as if it might solve it all.

He didn't bother to remove her undergarments, or any more of his clothes. He simply freed himself, moved her underwear out of the way and slid home. When he lifted her, she wrapped her legs around him, and in one thrust she came apart there in his arms, shaking and shuddering, his name on her lips.

It was wrong, and yet it felt as right as anything ever had. The soft give of her—fire for fire. Turning all this rage into something not so sharp, not so all-encompassing. Her hands in his hair, her body bowing to meet every desperate thrust.

"More," she demanded of him.

So he gave her more. He took her to that edge, flung her over it until she was weak with it, limp with it. A shuddering mass of everything he could do to her.

Him.

He roared out his release, and in the aftermath of it all, he knew he'd solved nothing. And yet he felt as though he'd solved it all.

CHAPTER THREE

SAVERINA HAD NEVER spent the night at Teo's place before. Though they often spent time here, in his bed, she usually she made her excuses somewhere near midnight, half hoping he'd ask her to stay, but he never did.

Last night, though, they'd worn each other out—over and deliciously over—and she'd dozed off before she could make her customary offer. So this morning she woke up tucked next to him, warm and sated and...happy.

It was a step, surely. Instead of shuttling her away, he'd let himself feel his feelings *with* her. That had to mean something. Something positive. She certainly felt *positive* this morning. Blissfully, pleasurably used and spent and worshipped.

She sighed into the memory, snuggled closer to his warm form. But he was a bit like a very hard, immovable furnace. Maybe he was still asleep, but she got the feeling he was awake. Lying there next to her. Making no effort to pull her close, to drop a kiss to her forehead, to do anything.

Almost as if…he didn't want her here. Almost as if last night was different for him than it was for her, no matter how many times they'd happily destroyed each other.

Saverina kept her breathing carefully even as anxiety began to creep in. He could have *told* her to go. He could have done a lot of things. So she wasn't going to catastrophize. She was going to open her eyes and be *happy*.

When she did, she noted he was in fact lying there wide awake. Staring at her. He had an expression on his face that reminded her of last night. Not angry, but all those things he put over the anger to hide them.

Happiness drained away quite quickly, anxiety seeping in easily, but she was a woman with pride. She did not let anything show in her expression, she hoped. She even smiled. "I'm sorry. I must have fallen asleep."

She made a move to roll away when he said nothing, but he held her there. So she could not make a casual slide out of bed and far away. She steeled herself to look over her shoulder and raise an eyebrow at him. Cool, regal, *sophisticated*. God, she hoped.

His gaze was as impenetrable as ever, but he made no move to let her go. Or to explain himself. Saverina, usually quick with a quip or *something* scathing, found herself…unable to find her voice. Everything felt too tenuous, like if she spoke or breathed or moved, it would all break and crash apart.

Maybe she should let it, but she didn't *want* to.

She wanted him to love her. Plain and simple. And she had never thought herself much like her mother, never understood her mother's destructive need to earn approval from a husband who was never going to give it.

Now, terrifyingly, Saverina thought she understood. But before she could do anything about it, Teo took in a deep breath, released her and got out of bed. "Do not go anywhere." Then he pulled on pants and strode out of the room, storms in his eyes.

He didn't seem angry as he had last night, but there was none of his usual smile or charms or easy way. Something was bothering him, eating at him, and it wasn't just the lawyer issue of last night. She was sure something darker simmered underneath *that* frustration. Which wasn't about her or wanting him to love her.

While he was gone, Saverina sat up in the bed, pulling the sheet around her as she was pretty sure all her clothes were out in the living room.

She didn't know what she was staying put for, what he was doing, but she didn't think she wanted to be completely uncovered to deal with it.

When he returned to the room, he was exactly the same. His pants were not fastened, he'd pulled on no shirt. His hair was wild.

From her hands.

There was *some* satisfaction in that as he approached the bed. She worked very hard to keep her cool expression in place, to give absolutely no hint of the way her heart was pounding in her chest or nerves had flooded every inch of her.

What *was* this? Was he…? Surely he wasn't going to break up with her while she sat here *naked* in his bed? The very thought had twin types of feelings rushing through her. Fear and pain and sadness so deep it threatened to make her cry.

And a roiling, dark, violent anger, the vicious temper handed down by her father that she worked very hard to keep on a leash.

Nevertheless, if he broke her heart right now, she'd *eviscerate* him, and she refused to feel an ounce of guilt over it. Sometimes fury *was* the answer. She just had to be careful about when that was and who it was aimed at.

But before she could say anything, tell him *all* that he'd be missing if he walked away from her, he knelt right next to the bed. This was strange enough, but then he held out his hand. He held a small box.

A jewelry box.

That pounding heart in her chest dropped straight down to her stomach, and she felt lightheaded, like all of her muscles had suddenly gone to jelly.

"Marry me," he said. Stern and earnest.

Saverina could only stare. He had a ring. Two simple words. *Marry me.* She thought she should want to jump at the chance, scream yes and throw herself at him. And part of her did, just as part of her was in the tears threatening to fall over.

Marry meant commitment. A life together. And she loved him, so much, she could admit to herself *now*. She could see wonderful and happy years stretched out together, making a family, just like so many of her siblings were doing.

But she didn't speak because something was… missing. It took her a moment to understand why it all felt a little…hollow, even with a symphony of other emotions running through her.

He offered no declarations of love. No promises of a future. Nothing soft at all. She didn't need over-the-top gestures, but was it wrong to want more than a demand to stay put, then a statement and a ring?

She didn't like being commanded, and she didn't like the nearly emotionless way this was all going down. A marriage proposal should be…about all that future they would make together. All the feelings that had led him here.

Shouldn't it?

She *wanted* to say yes. She *wanted* to marry him. To throw herself into all they were, but could she do that when he'd never once said he loved her? When no one around them even knew they were together? Was this leaping too far ahead, too quickly?

Her brain whirled in circles and still he just knelt there, ring outstretched, waiting for her answer like they had all the time in the world.

She looked into his dark eyes, but they gave nothing away. Like there was nothing inside. Like this was a business transaction. He wasn't nervous or excited or felled by love or even lust.

But last night hadn't been devoid of *feelings*. It had been full of them. Waking up to him meant something, it *had* to. And *she* loved him. He clearly cared for her or he wouldn't be proposing marriage. This was not her mother's experience. Saverina was too strong for all that.

So maybe she didn't *need* the words. Maybe, if she loved him and wanted to marry him and he was asking, the only thing to do was say yes. To take what she wanted.

Unless you're setting yourself up for unmitigated failure.

Saverina did not respond. She sat there, naked in his bed with the sheet wrapped around her. Tempting and beautiful and resolutely *silent*.

When he was altering his plans. All because he'd woken up to her gently asleep next to him like… He shook away the strange sensation he'd had with her tucked up against him, breathing quietly.

He'd thought to himself that she *would* be his bride, one way or another, so why wait any longer? Why not propose right now? Insist upon it after last night? Surely she'd fling herself headfirst into it the same way she'd flung into his anger—turning it into something else entirely. Renewal.

But she sat there now and said *nothing*. Gave away nothing. Frustration and anger started to mix with some other emotion he refused to acknowledge. Was this just another thing that would go wrong? Another wrench in his climb for revenge?

He wouldn't allow it.

"It is a yes-or-no question, *bedda*," he said, and

was quite happy with how smooth his voice came out sounding. Instead of as rough and frustrated as he felt.

She looked up from the ring, eyes cool but oddly bright like there might be tears in them. And something too close to fear for comfort. "It wasn't a question at all, Teo," she said in that crisp way of hers—a tone she usually only used at work. "It was a statement."

He smiled in spite of himself. Perhaps all his plans weren't ash after all. Perhaps Saverina with her cool command and insistence on being *asked* could be the shining star that saved it all. Before he had met her, he'd been so sure she would be weak-willed and naive, and only now, with so many of his plans within reach, did he realize that wouldn't do at all.

He needed her strength. Her poise. Even that little flash of temper he saw sometimes. She would be able to handle all that came with aplomb. Because she was perfect.

And so was his plan.

"Ah, my little *principessa* does not like a statement. *Scusa.*"

She got all prim-looking then, chin in the air, looking down her nose at him.

"So regal," he murmured, getting up off his knees because he'd be damned if he was going to grovel. He moved onto the bed next to her, ring still outstretched. He let the hand closest to her slide down her shoulder, over her elbow and to her hand, which he took in his while he worked to make sure he sounded…whatever way a man was supposed to sound when he did something as foolish as propose.

Gentle and besotted or some such. He lifted her hand to his mouth, pressed a kiss to her palm. "*Will* you marry me, Saverina?" he asked, infusing as much warmth into the *question* as he could manage.

She sucked in a breath, and for a moment, her expression went open, vulnerable. If he looked too deep, he saw a longing that had a twist of guilt vising his lungs. Which wouldn't do.

Thankfully, she blinked it away quickly, and then her lips slowly began to curve. She cleared her throat before she spoke. "Now, that's a question I think I can answer." She looked down at the box. The ring was flashy, expensive, and he'd thought it suited her personality the moment he'd seen it. She was not a shy woman, not afraid of demanding the attention of an entire room.

All those flashes of vulnerability and fear were figments of his imagination. Or his guilt. *This* was her. She would say yes, and he, in return, would ensure she had the best. He would treat her well. It did not need to be love or real to work. To be fair enough.

She smiled at him, all bright and far too…hopeful to land in him well. "Yes," she said, her voice little more than a whisper. "I'll marry you, Teo."

That vise on his lungs was back, but he ignored it. He was an expert at ignoring those unwanted, unwieldy feelings. Maybe it was dangerous to have them around Saverina, but he knew what he was about. He knew his goal.

So he pulled her forward, pressed his mouth to hers. And refused to sink into the soft promise of her. Because he had work to do. He pulled away. "We really shouldn't be late to work. Particularly both of us."

She glanced over at the clock, then waved it away. "I've got about ten minutes left to bask." She held the ring up and let it sparkle in the light of the room. She settled in against him, like casual intimacy would be a part of their future, when he had no plans for that to be the case.

He should stop this.

.He did not get up.

"We haven't even told my family or *anyone* we're dating," she said with half a laugh. "How am I going to explain this?"

"We don't have to tell them about the engagement straightaway." He had a timetable for when they needed to announce it by, but last night had given him more time on that score.

See? Not a mistake, not a failure, not even a misstep. His revenge would not be thwarted, because he had promised to enact it. Nothing would stop him. Not even a few setbacks. They would end up, always, working in his favor. One way or another.

Saverina laughed again, leaning her head against his shoulder, still admiring her ring. "I kind of love the idea of springing it on them with no warning, but Lorenzo and Brianna are away, and I'll want to get as many of them home as I can to tell them in person. So we'll keep it under wraps for now." She moved the ring from one finger to another so that it no longer denoted engagement. She stared at it for a moment, then looked up at him.

Teo had to swallow against the ocean of hope he saw there in her dark eyes.

"Are you sure about this? That this is what you want? Forever?" she whispered, tears sparkling. So unguarded he felt as though she'd cut him off at the knees. "I'm going to have to insist on forever if we're getting married."

He was not a good man, he reminded himself. Guilt and being cleaved in half did not matter if he got the necessary end result. The revenge he'd promised. The revenge Dante Marino deserved.

"Of course, I am sure."

He would have everything he wanted. Guilt be damned.

CHAPTER FOUR

BEING ENGAGED WAS strange when it was being hidden, because it was supposed to be something momentous, or so Saverina had always assumed. But nothing in her life had *really* changed. Even if she scanned wedding dress websites on her lunch break, or found herself thinking about cakes, flowers, color schemes, it was all internal.

Everything external remained the same. She'd even spent the past three nights at home rather than at Teo's after having dinner with him and enjoying his bed.

Which didn't bother her—she was refusing to let it bother her. She'd been the one to want to keep the relationship a secret, and now that meant the engagement had to be. She couldn't bear the thought of Lorenzo hearing about it from someone else. Maybe he was her older brother, but he'd also been the closest to a real father figure she'd ever had. And she wasn't fully sure how he'd take this.

He liked Teo—as an employee. He *never* liked secrets. So she would have to address this all...very carefully. Once he was back from his well-deserved holiday.

Teo respecting that, keeping this a secret with absolutely no pressure to do otherwise, was just another sign of the way he cared for her. Maybe she'd spent too much time the past few days fretting about why he'd never once uttered the words *I love you*, but she was too much of a coward to say them either, so maybe that was her fault.

Some people were bad with words, she told herself, night after night on her way home. She'd never considered Teo one of them, but…maybe it was deeper. Something to do with his mother, his childhood, some hidden trauma he'd never let her in on.

It didn't matter. Him saying the words didn't matter if he wanted to *marry* her. That was the same as love.

Wasn't it?

She thought about asking her sister-in-law when Lorenzo and Brianna called from their babymoon to check in, because Brianna obviously had experience with difficult men allergic to feelings. But she was too afraid of what Brianna might say. Like, *No, Saverina, he does not love you if he cannot say it.*

Or what Brianna might tell Lorenzo, Teo's *boss*.

She wasn't about to worry her other brothers or sisters over the conundrum as she much preferred everyone to think of her always in the driver's seat. She was on her own—the way she always was, because *she* chose it.

Besides, Brianna had once told her love was work,

not a fairy tale. So Saverina supposed that's all this was. The work Brianna had been talking about.

She decided to walk down to the sandwich shop for lunch, hoping the exercise would clear her head. Maybe it wouldn't be clear until she could tell her family. Maybe secrecy—which she'd rather enjoyed up to this point—was now more weight than fun.

Before she ordered her sandwich, she began to paw through her purse and realized she didn't have her wallet. She tried to think of the last time she'd had it. She'd bought dessert on the way to Teo's last night, wanting to surprise him with his favorite cannoli.

She must have left the wallet at Teo's when she set the dessert down. She wasn't usually so careless, but she recalled—with heat flaming into her cheeks—he'd arrived a few minutes after her, and she'd soon forgotten about both the wallet *and* her dessert surprise.

They'd made a dessert all their own.

She glanced at her watch. If she took a taxi, she could make it to Teo's, grab her wallet, and be back in her office before her lunch break was up. And hopefully cool the heat in her cheeks at the memory of last night's activities.

She smiled to herself as she hailed a taxi and gave the driver Teo's building's address.

See. Things were *good*. No need to feel confused. She should focus on the happiness, the excitement. Because she felt those too.

Of course, she felt a little…uncomfortable going

to Teo's apartment without his permission. But she had a key. She often was there without him if he was running late. It was not *unheard* of.

And she refused to ask her *fiancé* for permission to enter his place and look for *her* wallet. If he needed that, well, they were going to have a discussion about what it meant to join their lives together.

Shouldn't you have done that already?

She shoved that annoying little thought out of her head and pulled out her phone. She knew he was in a meeting, so she fired off a quick text.

On a search for my wallet. Headed to your apt. Need anything while I'm there?

There. Casual. Informative. Certainly not asking permission. And since he was occupied, he likely wouldn't answer until she was done.

She paid the driver, then walked into Teo's building, waving at the doorman and greeting the elevator attendant politely. They were all paid to be discreet in an apartment building such as this, so they knew her. Knew exactly where she was going. The attendant pushed the button to Teo's floor, and quickly enough, she was letting herself into Teo's apartment.

Feeling a bit like a burglar. Which was *ridiculous*. She marched straight for the kitchen, quickly finding her wallet. She slid it into her purse, and considered grabbing something from his fridge since she now didn't have time for lunch.

But then she heard an odd *ding*. Confused, she

moved out of the kitchen and looked around. Surely he hadn't left his phone or laptop behind, but if he had, she could always bring it to him. Maybe they were *both* out of sorts.

Because engagement was a *big* step, a life-changing one. Not because it was the wrong one, but simply because it was *momentous*.

There on the coffee table *was* a laptop. The screen had lit up with the ding. But it wasn't a Parisi computer. It was a personal one she'd never seen before.

None of her business, she told herself…even as she stepped toward the couch. He could, of course, have a laptop she'd never *once* seen him use. Why wouldn't he? She needed to head back before her lunch break ended.

She lowered herself onto the couch. The password window had come up with the *ding*, but in the corner was a banner with the subject and sender of the email that had come through.

Veritas Lab. DNA Sample Received.

She didn't breathe. For a moment, she just read the subject over and over and over. Then she forced herself to suck in air.

He was probably doing one of those silly ancestry tests. He never spoke of family besides his late mother. Maybe he was searching farther afield.

It would make sense.

What didn't make sense was worrying that it was

worse. That maybe he had a child out there. Maybe some woman was suing him for paternity. Maybe…

So many *maybes*.

And most of them were perfectly innocent *maybes*, so she should let this go. If it was something bad, he would tell her.

Unless he doesn't.

"You're being foolish," she whispered to herself. Out loud here in Teo's living room.

But that of course did not change the anxiety spiking inside of her.

She knew what would, though.

No one knew about her computer skills, certainly not Teo. Lorenzo knew she had *some* experience because even in university he'd kept up with what classes she was taking, what her grades had been. But he didn't know about her side hacking projects, all the below board things she'd learned off at university because computers were interesting and hacking could be fun.

She had kept quiet about that because she didn't think her family would approve, but also because if they knew her skill level, both Lorenzo and her other brother, Stefano, would pressure her to join the IT department at Parisi.

She didn't want that kind of pressure. The internet security of their entire livelihood? No. Too much room for error. For failing them.

But there was no pressure in seeing if she could get through Teo's private computer security. There was no pressure in seeing what he was keeping from her. There was only the moral issue.

It was wrong to poke through his personal computer. It was wrong to sift through whatever he might be keeping a secret, because he would tell her if it was important. She trusted him.

But if she reversed the situation, and she had *nothing* to hide, she would not care if he sorted through her things. Because secrets were dangerous. Secrets were poison. There had been so many secrets during her childhood—how her mother and sister had supported the family through prostitution, her father's drinking problem, her sister's death and the way Lorenzo had handled *everything*—carefully kept from her because she was the baby.

Too weak. Too delicate. Too whatever.

If Teo had a secret…she had to know. Fair or not, right or not, she *had* to know. So she hit the keystrokes necessary to hack into his system—beyond the password, the security, the files he'd saved encrypted. She set herself a deadline—allowing some time to be late from her lunch, but not so late as to raise eyebrows.

She scanned emails, documents for mentions of DNA. At first, it seemed he was just trying to find out the identity of his father—and though she knew he wasn't in Teo's life, she'd had no idea he didn't even know the man's *identity*.

She began to feel slimy and gross and wrong as she dug. She'd have to confess everything to him and hope he could forgive her for poking into his private—

And then she saw a name that had her entire body turning to ice.

Dante Marino.

Her brother's number one enemy. A man who had spent years trying to ruin Lorenzo—his company, his reputation, his family. Lorenzo mostly brushed it off these days—it was hard to make rumors stick when Lorenzo was so dedicated to his family and was careful with his hiring practices at Parisi.

But there was no way Dante had given up. None of the Parisis thought so, even if Lorenzo was particularly philosophical about the whole thing.

"Let him try to drag me through the mud," Lorenzo had once said. He'd been sitting with Brianna on one side of him. She'd been nursing their new daughter, Gio—his oldest, snug on his lap. *"I have everything I need."*

Saverina tried to keep that sweet, unbothered memory in her mind, but her blood was boiling.

The only conclusion she could draw to finding Dante's name in Teo's personal files was that Dante Marino had sent Teo LaRosa to hurt her family.

Her phone dinged, causing her to jump. Teo had replied to her text.

The only thing needed is you naked in my bed.

She stared at that text. So incongruous to the moment. Twenty minutes ago, it would have sent a bolt of heat through her—and she wasn't immune to the physical reaction of knowing what he could do with such a premise.

But now she had a sneaking suspicion as to *why*. He was connected to Dante somehow. He wanted to hurt her brother somehow, no doubt. *Through* her.

Teo had made her a pawn.

He'd made her a fool.

She signed out of the computer, put it back exactly the way it had been. He'd never know she touched it. He'd never know what she knew.

Because she would not confront him with this. No.

She would make him pay.

Teo was on cloud nine. Dante's DNA had finally been collected and dropped off with the testing site. He would have his proof within the week. Which meant he needed to get Saverina moving along on the relationship front.

He rather liked having her to himself, having everything be a secret so every night together felt like theirs and theirs alone.

But this was not the plan. The plan was revealing to everyone he was Dante's son. An illegitimate son—painting Dante the adulterer, child abandoner, which was bad enough.

But then, to twist the knife, show the Parisi family as his saviors. Lorenzo, the man who'd given him a chance to raise to the lucrative position he was at now. So kind and generous and *such* a family man he'd even allowed Teo to fall in love with his prized sister.

Media channels would eat it up, exaggerate it beyond the telling. Dante would forever be ruined—his traditional, family-friendly, upstanding reputation in tatters. While the Parisis soared.

Teo nearly laughed alone in the elevator. He needn't have worried last week. Everything was working out just as it should.

Not that he was getting cocky. He wouldn't do that again. Just that he'd enjoy each little step toward success.

For you, Mamma.

The thought of his mother was always sobering, but more than that these past few days, it seemed to twist into his mother *and* Saverina. They weren't much alike, but still he could see, if she'd lived, them enjoying each other's company. Saverina's sharp wit, his mother's kind soul. Saverina would have made her laugh. Mamma would have eased those strange hints of fear he sometimes saw in Saverina's eyes.

But it was of no matter. His mother was dead. Saverina's fears were her own.

And his plan was all that mattered. The elevator stopped at Saverina's floor—because he'd pushed that number. He strode out of the elevator when the doors opened, then stopped short, looked around, as if he hadn't meant to get out on this floor.

This was a farce they'd played a few times. He knew she rather liked it—the secrecy, the sneaking around. Now he hoped someone saw him. Saw a pattern. Began to wonder.

Because they would need to announce this engagement by the end of the month.

He looked down the hall to Saverina's desk, politely smiling at anyone who passed or made eye contact with him. Then he turned back to the elevator—once the doors had closed—and pushed the down button once more.

Like clockwork, Saverina exited her office. He didn't look her way, but in his peripheral vision, he watched her approach.

"Good afternoon, Ms. Parisi," he offered quietly when she came to stand next to him, as if also waiting for the elevator and *only* the elevator.

"Good afternoon," she replied.

When the doors opened, they stepped inside in tandem. He hit the lobby button, then waited for the doors to close before turning his grin on her.

But she did not look at him or sidle closer as she usually did.

Odd.

"Are you going to the charity gala the art society is hosting?" he asked, hoping she would enjoy his new plan. "We should go together. Not as an engaged couple, of course, but start moving the wheels toward the idea that we are indeed a couple."

She didn't say anything. Didn't meet his gaze. There was a frown on her face. The elevator doors would open soon, but still he could not resist, reaching over and brushing a hand over her hair.

"Are you feeling all right, *bedda*?"

She smiled up at him, and it was her normal smile, but something… Something in her eyes was not right. Like a dimming. "Just a migraine. I think I'll go home and lie in a dark room for the night." She looked down at her purse. "I know we had plans, but you don't mind, do you?"

The doors opened, and she stepped out first. He followed, dogged by a strange confusion. "Of course not." It would give him time to work on his timeline, his media contacts. Ensuring his whisper network never pointed back to him as the source, because that was just another way to twist the knife for Dante. Make it look like Teo himself had been willing to keep such a thing secret.

Saverina hadn't answered his question about the gala. And she strode toward the lobby doors with clear, quick purpose. So quick, he was practically tagging along after her even though his natural stride was much longer than hers.

They did not share goodbye kisses here at the office, but still something about the way she headed for her car without a goodbye or a smile left him feeling… concerned. Was she angry with him for some slight? Women, he supposed, were forever doing that sort of thing.

But before she fully reached her car, she turned and shaded her eyes against the setting sun to look at him.

"Lorenzo asked if I'd join them on the last leg of their trip. The children are wearing Brianna out."

"Do they not have nannies for that kind of thing?"

"I enjoy the children, and it would give me the opportunity to tell them about us. Explain everything so they don't think the engagement is too quick. I'd hate to have Lorenzo disapprove." Again she gave him that smile that was dimmed.

By the migraine, obviously. She was in pain. It made sense. And she was talking of breaking the news of the engagement to the person keeping that news from being spread far and wide, so this was good. Once Lorenzo knew, the plan could move forward. "I hope you have a wonderful time, then. When do you leave?"

"Early tomorrow morning."

This shocked him, and he didn't think he did a very good job of hiding it. Because her smile changed, Sharpened, ever so slightly.

"I'm sorry for the short notice," she said. She lifted a hand, and for a moment he thought she would reach out. Offer something physical with her goodbye.

But she only made an odd waving motion. "I'll text," she offered, then turned to her car. She slid into the driver's seat and closed the door behind her. No extra smiles. Nothing.

He found himself watching the car drive away. Unsettled. Frustrated. With the strangest sensation battering his chest and the errant and incomprehensible thought that he'd miss her while she was gone.

CHAPTER FIVE

SAVERINA DID NOT go to meet Lorenzo and Brianna on their vacation. That had never been the plan. Subterfuge was the plan.

Crushing Teo LaRosa was the plan.

She called off work for the week and spent the next few days hacking into Teo's personal and professional emails and systems to gather more information, but she was still mostly left with the fact Teo was DNA testing to see if Dante Marino was his father. And he had befriended quite an array of media professionals over the past year—mostly from anonymous accounts.

She wasn't quite sure how or if these things connected, but they were the only two facts she could be certain of from his digital communication.

She found no evidence Teo and Dante had ever spoken, but she could think of no other reason for a connection to her family's enemy than that Teo was working *against* Parisi. She found no evidence Teo had done anything to hurt Parisi on a professional level, so corporate espionage seemed a bit of a stretch.

After a few days, she accepted she'd scoured every computer avenue—now she had to do some real-life digging. She needed more information before she knew how to proceed. How to crush Teo into tiny, jagged, destroyed bits and wished he'd never even *looked* at her, let alone fooled her.

She'd considered hiring someone to follow him, but she hadn't been able to get over the desire to hear it herself. From his own mouth, whatever he was trying to do to her family. So tonight, she would set out to follow him herself.

Maybe he would recognize her, maybe it would destroy her revenge, but she needed to do this herself.

Her fury wouldn't allow anything else. Besides, she had some experience trying to move through the world without being seen. When she'd been at university and Lorenzo's false misdeeds had been plastered about, she'd wanted to keep a low profile, and she had. All it took, often enough, were baggy clothes, an unflattering hairstyle, and making certain to engage eye contact with no one.

If she failed in this, there would be other ways to get answers, to thwart him, to ruin him. She was an intelligent woman with computer skills and a hefty trust fund and well-paying job. She would use every privilege in her arsenal to eviscerate the man who'd broken her heart.

She waited at the little restaurant patio across from Teo's apartment that evening, picking at a salad and waiting for him to arrive home. He did not have anything on his digital work calendar, but he'd had a little note on his personal one. No time. No date. Just an untitled entry.

She was going to find out what it was.

She had expected to be bored to death, waiting around, but she was so twisted up with anger and a hot, dangerous sense of purpose that watching for his car's arrival felt like watching a movie.

When he finally appeared, sliding out of the slick luxury car and waving off the valet, she felt a surge of too many conflicting emotions to wade through. If he didn't have the valet park his car in the garage, he was planning to come back out and use the car again.

He was so tall, so sure and handsome. It twisted inside of her hard and sharp, like grief, when the only thing she would allow herself was fury.

Besides, why should she grieve a love that was a *lie*?

He disappeared for half an hour, and in those ticking minutes, she pictured walking across the street and slapping him when he came down. Going up to his apartment with sultry smiles and dirty invitations— just to see if she could sway him from his purpose. She pictured herself doing all sorts of things, and every little daydream ended in his embarrassment and begging her forgiveness.

Perhaps if she had not watched her brothers conduct business with cool clarity, she might have indulged in any of those flights of fancy. But that was not how you won.

Clearheaded thought, follow-through, and surety were how you won.

When Teo reappeared, she paid her bill by leaving cash on the table and moved swiftly to her own car—well, Brianna's car, which she was borrowing. When Teo pulled out of his parking spot, she did so as well. She wondered if he'd be paranoid enough to notice Brianna's run-of-the-mill "mom car" tailing him.

She wasn't sure she cared. Part of her almost *hoped* he noticed. Confronted her. Part of her was dying to cause a scene.

But they drove through the glitzy, nicer parts of Palermo to the rougher back alleys. To a hole-in-the-wall bar she'd never been to. It was hard to picture Teo spending much time in this rough establishment either, but then again, she didn't know him.

He was a *liar*. A fake. A rat.

She waited in her car for a good ten minutes after Teo went inside before she got out of her car, and then took time to lock her car, check her reflection in the window, waste time until she saw a group of large men approach the door. She hurried her steps so that she could enter the bar, hidden behind their bulky forms.

Inside, she immediately spotted Teo even though the room was dark. He was sitting at a table in the corner, eyes on the door. But if he could see her through the crowd of men, his eyes passed right over her—likely thanks to the baggy clothes and her hair back in a braid that hid her usual soft waves—which was why she never wore it like this.

She kept her body as much behind larger men as possible as she worked her way through the crowd. She had a target. A booth right behind Teo's table. She would have to walk by him—so close he could reach out and touch her—but his gaze was so hard on the door that she decided she could take the risk.

She edged around the table, keeping her face tilted away, and calmly slid into the booth close enough to be in earshot.

He didn't even glance her way. His gaze never left the door. He was clearly waiting for someone very specific.

She let out a slow breath and stared hard at the wall. Her back was to him now, so she could not see him. Could not do anything but sit here and wait and hope that when his meeting partner came, she would be able to hear their conversation over the buzz of voices and the steady thrumming bass of the music playing over the speakers.

"You sure you want to wait for your friend?" a woman's voice asked. Saverina didn't twist in her seat, but she carefully angled her head so she could see Teo's table out of the corner of her eye.

A waitress was leaning over, trying to entice Teo to order something. Flirtatiously. Saverina watched, stomach twisting in knots, expecting him to smile, flirt, or charm her right back.

He did not. He ordered two drinks—clearly to get the waitress to leave him be—his gaze never leaving that door.

It didn't matter whether he was flirting back or

not, so she would *not* be relieved. They would never, ever be together now. He could entertain himself with as many women as he pleased.

And damn her breaking heart for throbbing there in her chest like a weak virginal *youth* at the thought.

She sucked in a breath, focused harder on the wall, and reminded herself what all this was for. For her brother. For the Parisi name. For *herself.*

"You're late." Teo's voice, low and cutting.

Saverina dared a look over at the table. A large man sat across from Teo now.

"Here are the results." The man slid a large envelope across the table. "They are what you hoped. How do you want me to proceed?"

She watched his profile as Teo took the envelope. He sucked in a breath, but no real emotion showed on his face. Knowing him made it clear to her that whatever was in the envelope was of the utmost importance to him.

"I'll deliver copies of this report to you when we're ready to go public. You'll distribute it to your contacts to go far and wide. It cannot get back to me."

"It won't."

"Then let's raise our glasses in a toast," Teo murmured. "To the destruction of Dante Marino." Teo's smile was cutting and harsh. His eyes glittered with that revenge he'd spoken of.

Not against Lorenzo and her family, but against her own enemy.

Saverina looked back at the wall, trying to understand…any of this. He wanted to destroy Dante.

Who was…his father, apparently, because getting revenge on a man whose DNA did *not* match didn't make sense. So, this was about his parentage? He was Dante's illegitimate son, and wanted some kind of revenge over that?

Perhaps she should be relieved, but she couldn't quite get there. Why was he tricking her when they wanted the same thing? Surely he knew she'd be more than happy to see Dante crushed. Nothing about this fit any of the scenarios she'd come up with in her mind, and she had *no* idea how to proceed.

Leave, and regroup. That was what she had to do. But before she could even think about getting up, someone slid into the booth across from her.

Teo.

She could only stare at him. No words, no excuses, no *thoughts* formed.

"I hope you heard all of that, *bedda*," he murmured silkily. "I'd hate to have to go over it again."

Teo would give her credit. Saverina didn't wilt when he slid into the booth across from her. She didn't look the least bit abashed. She looked coolly furious once she got over her shock.

And beautiful.

He couldn't think about that just yet. Too many things were problematic now. He wished he'd noticed her just a few minutes earlier, but he'd already made his toast when he'd caught sight of her profile in the booth.

How she'd gotten there, what she was doing, he

did not yet now. But he knew he had to play his cards very carefully.

His revenge would not be thwarted by her now.

She met his gaze, chin up and regal. All icy princess. Something painful twisted in his chest. He wanted to reach out. Touch the soft velvet skin of her cheek. Press his mouth to hers. He hadn't tasted her in days, and no matter how Dante and revenge had absorbed his every waking hour, he hadn't been able to put her out of his mind.

Unacceptable.

"I heard enough, I think, but not enough to understand quite what this is."

"I guess that's something we have in common this evening, because I cannot fathom why you are here, Saverina. When you told me you were away." When she should know nothing about his connection to Dante.

For a moment, she only held his gaze with a blank one of her own. "I suppose I never told you how much I abhor secrets, Teo. How I would go to any lengths to find the truth when I suspect I or my family might be in danger."

"I pose no threat to your family, Saverina."

"Anyone who connects to Dante Marino is a threat to my family, and apparently you have quite the connection."

He could not fathom how she had found this out, but he gave none of his surprise away. He thought he should be furious, but there was a different sensation plaguing him, and he did not understand it.

A kind of relief laced with pride. She knew, so he did not have to keep twisting the lies and secrets around someone who was now in so much of his life. She knew, because she was keen and smart and strong enough to suss out any threat.

But he was no threat.

"My revenge on Dante has nothing to do with our relationship—"

"Don't." And she sounded just hurt enough under the icy fury that he could not continue the lie he'd always meant to tell her if she began to have suspicions about his motives. "Perhaps I don't understand what you're after, or why you'd use me to get it, but I know you were using me. It is not *coincidence*. Your job at Parisi. Your engagement to me."

"You don't know that."

"I do. Because you don't love me, Teo. That is very obvious."

"Then why did you agree to marry me?"

For a moment, he saw those vulnerable hurts of hers he was forever pretending weren't there because they so quickly disappeared. Tonight, she simply looked down. "I thought... I came here tonight because I thought your connection to Dante was about hurting my family."

"I have no wish to hurt your family, Saverina." Not that he had any plans to *protect* them, either. It just happened they had the same enemy, so they could all give each other things they wanted.

She nodded. "Well, that is a relief. But you're

going to have to explain to me what your plans *are*, or I am going to have to make some of my own."

"Like what?"

She met his gaze, and he did not wish to recognize any of the feelings swirling in there. So he did not.

Then her gaze dropped to her hand. She pulled the ring he'd given her off and pushed it across the table toward him.

He stopped her forward movement with his hand over hers. "Let us not be hasty," he murmured. "Why don't we return home and—"

"Do you think I would marry you now?" she asked. "You must be delusional. Your best option at this juncture is to convince me not to tell Lorenzo everything I know, and so far you are failing in that."

Temper poked, Teo smiled and leaned back in his booth. He left her hand and his ring right there at the center of the table as he looked down at her with as much disdain as he could muster. "Ah, yes, run home to Daddy, is it?"

Everything in her expression sharpened—anger, disgust, hate. He welcomed them all. Better than hurts and vulnerabilities that poked at things he dared not look directly at.

"You are an adult, Saverina," he said, keeping all the scathing in his tone. "Behave as one. Think this through. Dante has hurt your family. Now, I can get my revenge on him alone, for just myself. I have no issues doing such. But won't it be better, more satisfying, if we work together to destroy him? Once and for all."

He thought she might look shamed or hurt, but she leaned back in the booth as he did. His ring—which likely cost more than everything in this bar—sat on the sticky table between them.

She raised a regal eyebrow, crossed her arms over her chest. He should have known she would not be so easy to mold. "You have me confused with someone else, Teo." Then she slid out of the booth as if she owned this entire low-end bar and sauntered out of the establishment, with more than a few eyes watching the sway of her hips as she left.

CHAPTER SIX

SAVERINA BLINKED BACK tears as best she could. The evening outside the bar was cool and dark, and she wanted nothing more than to make it to the car and sob all the way home.

Everything was a lie. She'd known this for days now, but something about having to deal with Teo, something about it being not quite the betrayal she had thought it was, made all her defenses crumble.

But she heard footsteps behind her, and she would be damned if she would cry in front of this scheming, lying, horrible *bastard*. She sucked in a breath and blew it out hard, then turned to face him. She shook her hair back, looked up into his dark flashing eyes.

His expression was one she'd never seen before— except that night he'd come home angry. The night they'd…

She could not think about all the ways she'd let this man into her heart.

"I am not through with you, Saverina," he growled.

"What a shame for you." She jerked her car door open, unsurprised when he grabbed it and blocked her entrance. She didn't rage—though she wanted to. She met his fire with ice. "I'm not sure it would be a good look if I called the police, Teo. A harassment charge would certainly complicate your plans, I would think. Or is this a bit like father like son?"

It landed like a blow, as she'd hoped, and half feared would not. He was so smooth, so totally in charge, even when she'd clearly uncovered a secret he hadn't wanted uncovered. But *that* comment hit where it hurt. It flashed in his eyes, in the way his mouth went slack for just a moment.

She curled her hands into fists and assured herself it was *satisfaction* she felt at the arrested look on his face.

Quickly smoothed away.

"I could turn this on you, *bedda*. I could make things equally as uncomfortable for Parisi as I do for Marino."

A threat? She wanted to *laugh*. "And I could *destroy* you, and your sad little plan for revenge," she returned, unable to hold on to her ice. She *seethed*.

For a moment, they only stared at each other in the dim, unflattering parking lot light.

"I see we are at an impasse," he finally said. Cool and in control, which made her want to rage. But she held on to the tiny thread of composure she had left.

"Why don't we talk this through somewhere less public and more comfortable?" he said, as if this were a reasonable suggestion. As if they were in a boardroom. As if he was her *boss*.

"Follow me back to—"

"I will never step foot in your apartment again." Maybe it was showing her hand too much, but she knew he had the upper hand if they went back to his place. She wanted to believe herself immune, but if she went back to where they'd created far too many memories together, she was afraid she'd soften—to him, to his plan, to the chemistry between them.

She refused. But she couldn't ignore the fact his plan of destroying Dante Marino was...intriguing. Especially if it helped Parisi. Especially if Lorenzo never knew. She should likely send Teo off right now, but if there was a chance she could cut Dante Marino off at the knees... "If you simply must continue this fool's errand, then you can meet me at my house."

"Your brother's house."

She didn't even falter. "Yes, indeed."

"If I am seen at Lorenzo's home with you, people will talk. And they will talk in a direction that helps *my* plans."

"How shortsighted of you to think so," she returned. "You can either meet me there or not." She shrugged, jerked the car door out of his grip and slid into the driver's seat. She half expected him to try to keep her from closing the door, but he didn't.

Perhaps her threat to call the police was enough to keep him in line, but she doubted it. As she drove back the Parisi estate, she noted Teo followed in his own car very closely.

When she pulled through the gates, she clicked the button to keep them open for Teo's car, then drove around the twisting lane toward the garden—rather than the main house or her private entrance in the back.

No one would see his car here, and even if they did, they would not tell anyone except maybe Lorenzo. She wanted to keep as much of this from Lorenzo as possible, but if she had to tell her brother a version of events, she would.

She parked and slid out of the car. The moon and stars shone above. The smell of earth and flowers in the cool night air should have made this all a very romantic setting. She almost regretted never sneaking Teo in here back when...

When what? When he'd been lying to her? Talking her into his bed even though he had no feelings for her whatsoever? She had to breathe through her fury to keep herself from slamming her car door. Instead, she closed it quietly and moved over to the little bench among the plants and statuary.

Teo followed suit, though he did not sit with her on the bench—smart man. He stood before her, hands in his pockets, studying her like he'd never seen her before.

"I'll admit, the idea of destroying Dante Marino has me intrigued," she said, copying what she'd always called Lorenzo's *boardroom* voice. Not complimentarily, of course. Usually she was poking fun at him.

But the cold, detached way her brother spoke in business meetings would certainly help her conduct *this* one. Because that was all it was now. Business. The business of revenge.

"I cannot understand how tricking me into an engagement is part of such a plot, though. So why don't you enlighten me?" She looked up at him, hoping all the aching hurts swirling inside of her were hidden behind the wall of fury.

She half expected him to argue with her use of the word *tricking*. When he did not, she had to admit to herself that she'd *hoped* he'd argue with the word. It hurt that he didn't. That he launched into an explanation instead.

"I have spent the years since my mother's death perfecting my plan. And it *is* perfect. This is what we will do." He spoke as if there was no question that she would hop into this *we*. But he kept on, so clearly impassioned she couldn't even interrupt to correct him.

"We will announce our engagement. We will enjoy *that* attention for a short period of time before the rest begins to leak. People digging into my past. Into who I am. And slowly but surely, an image of a Dante Marino will emerge. A new image. A man who refused to acknowledge the son he created after coercing an employee. Who threatened her with his considerable power and privilege to never reveal a thing. He did everything he claims to stand against. Not just in the past, but now, when he refused to even see me."

"So… I'm just a plant to get people interested in you, Teo?" Had she really expected this to not make her feel worse and worse? Had she really expected this to *ease* things? She was a fool, but she'd never let him know she thought so. "How sad for you that you are that boring without me."

He didn't even spare her a quelling glance. "Expand your imagination, Saverina. While people are digging into my past—regardless of *you* and having everything to do with our impending union—it will be made quite clear through my many media contacts that while Dante ignored me, threatened my mother, made our lives hell—Parisi welcomed me with open arms. A job. A family. So much so that when I fell in love with the youngest Parisi, nothing but approval, welcoming, and acceptance was given to me. And everyone, finally, will see that Parisi is everything Marino isn't."

Too many emotions battered her then. She couldn't believe a heart could feel this bruised over someone she'd been involved with for a short time. How stupid she'd been to let him in there in the first place. How stupid she was to let her next words slip out. "That is the first time you've used that word. *Love*."

He had no quick response to that. She didn't dare look at him, too afraid she would feel his pity. Too afraid this failure would swallow her whole. Because it was a failure on her part. To believe a liar. To fall in love with one.

Her chest got tight, not just in pain but in that telltale sign she was heading for a panic attack. If anyone ever found out she'd been so fooled, if her siblings found out she'd been so *stupid*. That she'd failed so spectacularly. That...

She took in a breath through her nose, counted

to three. She used all the tools her university therapist had taught her for dealing with her panic. She would not lose her composure in front of *this* man.

"Why do you care about Parisi?" she managed to ask him, though she felt her tight throat and heard the strangled way she spoke a bit like she was floating up above herself.

"Because Dante cares. And wishes to see your family destroyed. Destroying him isn't enough for what he did to my mother. I will see his enemies lauded, his business ruined and handed over to his rival, while his reputation is ruined beyond the telling. I want everyone he hates dancing on the grave of the Marino name."

She breathed deep a few more times, stemming the tide. For now. It made a strange kind of sense, she supposed. How did you hurt someone irreparably? Not just take away everything he held dear—for Dante, his reputation—but also give his enemies everything he wanted. That positive media attention. That lauding. Any clients Marino lost would go to Parisi, no doubt.

The engagement to Teo wouldn't be real anymore—not that it ever had been, but now it would be an act for her as well as him. Could she go through with it? Was she that good an actress? Could she set her curdled feelings about Teo aside if it meant Dante Marino would get what he deserved? Perhaps he had not hurt Lorenzo the way he'd hurt Teo's mother, but he had tried to ruin Lorenzo's reputation, Lorenzo's business. All because Lorenzo had stood up to him.

Saverina breathed in through her nose, out through her mouth. Counted. Calmed. She didn't know if she could do this, but she knew she wanted to try. But first, she had to know… "Tell me one thing. What was the plan if I never found out?"

Teo had lies. Contingency plans for everything that was happening. Yet looking at her now, he struggled to voice them. He realized he wasn't quite as sure as he once had been that she would believe them.

He knew she was quick and sharp, but he supposed he'd still underestimated just *how* much. He wanted to find it annoying. A speed bump. But mostly he was impressed.

And other things he didn't want to acknowledge. Other things that reminded him too much of the days around his mother's death. Helplessness and failure and grief.

No, those feelings didn't belong here. "There was no plan. I would have been a husband to you. A good one at that. We would have had a perfectly nice life together. I have no need for a real marriage, no belief in things like love. So why not have it be a business arrangement?"

"While *I* thought it was love?"

He would not touch that question with a ten-foot pole. "There is chemistry between us, Saverina."

"Ah. A woman in your bed at your disposal was one of the things that wasn't a *lie* in this whole debacle. How comforting."

"I could have many a woman at my disposal should I so choose, *bedda*."

"But you chose me. For my last name. This is not quite the compliment you seem to think it is."

He scowled because she was taking this off the rails. While *he* was being reasonable and rational. "Regardless of how you feel on the matter, this was the plan. This *is* the plan. And you are here listening to it because you want to see Dante suffer almost as much as I do."

She frowned a little, but she did not argue. Because she wanted this too. Maybe he'd have preferred her to be in the dark. Maybe that would have been easier. It certainly would have given him more control over the situation, but nothing needed to change just because she knew. He still had his plan. He still had her.

Now he just needed his revenge.

He held out the ring she'd left on the table. "Things do not need to change, Saverina. We want the same things. It only involves a few well-placed pretends, and while we pretend, I can offer you anything you want."

She let out one of those odd long breaths, like a swimmer gasping for air. Yet she was perfectly calm and in control when she spoke. "No, you can't."

"Name it."

"Love, Teo. I want to marry someone I *love*. Like Lorenzo and Brianna love each other. They make each other happy. They make each other *better*."

He turned away from her then. His only experience with love was that it hurt. That it meant loss—

of control, of hope. He had loved his mother—and to what end? There had been nothing he could do to stop Dante from ruining her life. Nothing he could do to stop cancer from ending her life. Love did not matter. It was the most inconsequential thing on the planet.

"Love is what I want, and that is what you cannot give," she said.

Before he could think of anything to say to that ridiculousness, she stood and moved around so they were facing each other once again. She reached out, and he nearly backed away. He did not want to feel the soft brush of her comforting touch in this disorienting moment with the word *love* echoing about.

But she only uncurled his clenched fingers and took the ring from his hand. "But I also want to see Dante suffer for what he's done to Lorenzo. And since Lorenzo won't wage this war himself, I will. We will fake this engagement, Teo. I will play along with your plans. But I will not marry you. Once we have destroyed Dante, we will dissolve the engagement in a way that does not reflect poorly on either of us. That is the offer I'll extend to you. It's the only one I will, and you must decide now."

He surveyed this woman he could not seem to get a handle on. He didn't think he'd underestimated her, exactly. He'd known she was clever and might, at some point, begin to wonder about his motives, but he'd never expected her to understand his plan so quickly.

He'd never expected all the flashes of something

else in her expression to exist, or to bother him. To have him hesitating. It would be easy enough to lie again. To agree to her little counterplan knowing he had every inclination of talking her out of dissolving anything—for a few years at least.

But he was beginning to see that even if he could *persuade* her, that route came with…uncomfortable and unusual pitfalls.

"I cannot agree to this plan, as I think a marriage will be necessary to prove my point, to twist the knife. However, I will concede that the matter shall be left up in the air. If you can convince me a dissolution of our engagement can work once enough time has passed, I'll agree."

"And if not? I'll just be *required* to marry you?"

Teo lifted a shoulder. "I see no other way."

"You are ridiculous, Teo. I am in charge of saying 'I do.' Well, in this case, *not* saying it."

The sparring put him back on even ground. Re-cemented his control. He even managed a smile. "If you are so certain, there is no harm in agreeing, Saverina."

"There will be ground rules," she said fiercely. "*Reams* of them."

"You may come up with whatever rules you wish," he returned, and his smile got more genuine by the second.

She only scowled. "You must follow them."

"We'll see." Which he figured was a perfect time to make an exit. Let her consider it overnight. She would come to his way of thinking.

And if she didn't, he would simply convince her. Because they were as close to Dante's ruination as he'd ever been. So there was no turning back.

CHAPTER SEVEN

SAVERINA HAD KNOWN she would not sleep well. After she had finally accepted that she would not sleep at all, she'd gotten up and begun her list of ground rules.

The first thing she wrote down was the most important.

No physical contact unless expressly required to prove a point in a public setting.

She knew it gave away the fact that his touch affected her even after finding out his secret, but no doubt he already knew that. Protecting herself was more important than her pride in this *one* instance.

She was taking a risk, and she tended to avoid those, but if she failed in front of Teo… Did she care? He didn't matter to her—not anymore. Not the way her family did. So the most important thing to remember about all this was that as long as her family remained in the dark about her failures, everything would be okay.

She told herself this, over and over again. Through her lists of rules, through her morning routine of getting ready. She went down to breakfast and missed her brother and his little family because the noise would have distracted her from all the things twisting inside of her.

It was probably best they were enjoying their vacation, far away from what she was doing. She went to work, focused on the necessary tasks for her morning. Then, when it was time for her lunch break, she took the elevator up to Teo's floor.

She could have forwarded him the memos via email, but she'd printed them out because she wanted to deliver her carefully written rules to him—in as public a place as she could manage—without raising any eyebrows. So he understood she was serious, that *he* had to toe *her* line.

Mrs. Caruso eyed her as she approached. "Mr. LaRosa is very busy today."

Saverina smiled. "I'm sure. I only need to speak with him for a moment, and was hoping to catch him on his way out to lunch." Saverina made a rather over-the-top production of looking at her watch. "He *is* about to be on his way to lunch, isn't he?"

Mrs. Caruso only scowled, but she didn't stop Saverina from approaching Teo's office door or stepping inside. Since it wasn't a meeting, she didn't close the door behind her.

Or because you're a coward.

He sat behind his desk, gazing at his computer. He didn't even look up at her as she walked in. Which was good because her footsteps faltered for a moment. How could she still look at him and think he was breathtakingly handsome? How could she sit here and think about how his hair would feel if she raked her fingers through it after what he'd done?

She *hated* him. When was her body going to accept that?

"I have a few memos Lorenzo asked me to forward to you," she said, probably too loudly, moving toward his desk. Once she was close enough to speak quietly so her voice wouldn't carry to his likely listening assistant, she whispered, "And my list of ground rules."

This caught his attention. He flicked her a glance, then got to his feet. "Perhaps you could read them to me on our way to lunch." He moved around his desk and began to stride for the door.

Saverina stayed exactly where she was. "I cannot go to lunch with you in public," she said in another whisper that just barely avoided being a hiss.

"Why not? It is time, Saverina." He stalked back toward her until she had to lift her chin and remind herself she was *strong*, lest she back away or scramble behind his desk just to put space between them. Just to be able to breathe the same air as him.

Because of *rage*, she assured herself. That was the heart-pounding, pulse-quickening sensation moving through her. Whatever vestiges of attraction she felt for him, they were just mixed up with all this distaste for him. And they would fade.

Wanting to touch him had to fade.

"We must begin to set the stage," he said quietly. "Lunch today. The gala this weekend. You may tell your family we've been seeing each other whenever and however you wish. My gift to you."

Gift. While he was standing there telling her what to do like *he* was in charge. "Have you always been this arrogant?"

"Of course. You just thought it was charming when you wanted it all to be real."

The dig hurt, but she looked at his easy expression and knew he didn't even *mean* it to be a dig. In his world, it was just a truth. Because he felt no shame for what he'd done. For how he'd tricked her. He didn't even fully understand *why* lying the way he had would hurt her.

She honestly did not know what to do with that. Had no one ever taught him right from wrong? Was he so blinded by revenge that he just couldn't consider it might be *wrong* to use her? Was he so unaccustomed to love he couldn't fathom it could hurt when it wasn't reciprocated?

She did not know. Wasn't sure she wanted to.

Then he took her by the arm. She narrowly resisted jerking out of his grasp. Instead, she carefully and coolly stepped to the side so his hand had to either tighten or drop.

It dropped. "It seems there are a few rules we must go over *before* lunch, Teo. First, you will not touch me." She set the memos she'd brought on his desk and held out the piece of paper with her carefully written and considered list of rules.

He sighed. Heavily. Then took the offered piece of paper. His eyes skimmed over the writing.

"So, you will not come to my apartment under any circumstances," he summarized. "We will not be alone together—anywhere. I must run all plans by you before I do anything." He fixed her with a pity-ing gaze. "Come, Saverina, you do not really expect me to follow these foolish attempts at control. *I* am in the driver's seat. This is *my* plan."

"One you need me for."

"Very well. I will agree to let you in on all the plans you're a part of before I enact them. I will keep my hands to myself, and under no circumstances in-vite you back to my apartment." He handed her the list and smiled, slow and devastating. "Even when you beg me to do just that."

She was so shocked—because clearly her entire body heating through and through was *shock*—that her mouth hung open, and no pithy retort came out.

"Come. We can argue over lunch. We will walk down to the restaurant on the corner. Sit on the patio." He walked toward the door, glanced over his shoulder and raised an eyebrow when she did not follow. "You do want to hear the rest of my plan, do you not? Put your stamp of approval on it."

A stamp of approval he clearly did not want or need. He was going to keep steamrolling right along.

Well. She was going to find a way to put a stop to that. Or at least keep one step ahead of him. This lunch wasn't it, but she didn't know how to say no. If this plan was to work, they *did* need to start going public.

And she would need to explain to her brother that

she was dating one of his top executives in Palermo. So that when she announced her engagement, Lorenzo wouldn't *totally* flip.

She followed Teo out to the hall.

"I will be on my lunch for the next hour, Mrs. Caruso," he told his assistant. He glanced at Saverina. "If you would hold my calls, I'll get back to anyone upon my return." He smiled at Saverina, that devastatingly charming smile she'd once fallen for.

Now he did it in clear view of Mrs. Caruso, who frowned. But voiced no argument.

Saverina didn't want to think about how that might have thrilled her just a week ago. How she would have taken it as a sign of his *love*. It made her entire stomach turn.

"If we are to be believed, Saverina," he murmured as they stepped into the elevator, "you're going to have to stop looking like you've swallowed a lemon."

She glared at him as the doors closed. "Pretending not to hate you is going to take a level of acting that would win me an award."

"Ah, but you do not hate me. You're not a hateful person, Saverina. Perhaps you'd like to be, but you're too...soft."

"Soft?" It was so ludicrous, she scoffed. Which helped wipe the scowl from her face as they left the elevator for the lobby. "I suppose believing you listened to me was just another fiction."

"I listen."

The serious way he said those words made her shiver, but she fought through the feeling as they stepped into the sunshine. He was lying. Everything about him was a lie.

And now that she knew, she'd never forget.

Teo arranged for a table out on the patio, in a corner and a little bit away from the other tables so they could speak freely. He wanted to be seen, and he liked the way the afternoon light dappled Saverina's dark hair. The patio was quite full as it was a pretty, sunny day. The sidewalks just outside were bustling with people. But they had their own corner.

Once they were seated and had ordered their lunches, Saverina looked around. "If anyone we know sees us, they will only assume it's a working lunch."

"Will they?" He leaned forward, did his best impression of a besotted fool—a look he'd seen her brother give his wife more times than he liked to count. "Perhaps your no-touching rule will make it more difficult to get my point across, but you'd be surprised what people will read into the right kind of *look*."

She angled her chin away from him. He didn't bother scolding her for not *acting* like they were on a date. He might need her to exude something less edgy and angry to convince people they were *happily* together, but telling her what to do wasn't working quite the way he'd imagined it would.

He'd need a new strategy. "Tell me how your weekend was, Sav."

She scowled at him, presumably for shortening her name—so that was not the strategy. Clearly.

"We aren't friends, Teo. I see no reason to *pretend* we are."

"Ah, but the enemy of my enemy *is* my friend. Particularly in this case."

She shook her head and took a sip of water. She wore a yellow top today, buttoned up practically to her chin. Like she'd known she'd see him and wanted to keep as much of her body covered as she could.

It gave him a strange kind of thrill. He supposed because it meant she thought about how he could make her body feel. Her no touching and no alone time "rule" also pointed to the fact that while she might be frustrated with him, angry that he'd lied to her and kept things from her, she still wanted him.

He studied her now. She would be in his bed again—willingly and happily. He had no doubt. Once she got over her somewhat childish hurt, she would realize that their situation was much better than any sort of *love*.

"Well, I spent much of my week hacking into all your systems, discovering you to be a scheming liar, and then confronting you about it, so it was quite full."

"Ah, but you did not confront me, Saverina. I caught you." But it brought up an interesting point. How she'd gotten the information she had. Hacking. He studied her. Was his Parisi princess *that* skilled? "You're claiming to have gotten into my personal computer?"

"And phone. And tablet. Basically anything you've ever connected to your network—or Parisi's."

She said it so conversationally, he frowned. "My security is quite solid."

"I'm sure you think so. I'm sure the Parisi's IT department thinks so as well. But it only takes one person with a decent enough set of skills and a target to get through all that *solid* security."

Wasn't she a delightful surprise? If all this was true... He leaned forward, lowered his voice. "Could you hack into Marino's systems?"

She didn't say anything at first, didn't look at him, but he saw the flare of interest in her eyes. The subtle relaxing of her shoulders. When she finally met his gaze, hers was cool. But he saw the eagerness. "It wouldn't be the first time. Why didn't *you* hire someone to do it before?"

"I'd considered it, but in the end I didn't find anyone with the necessary skills who was also as trustworthy as I preferred. Surely I can trust you, Saverina."

She smirked. "We'll see, I suppose."

She really was a delight. Their meals were set in front of them, and he watched as she picked at hers. Not wearing that frown that did something uncomfortable to his insides. More like wheels were turning in her head. "I never found anything damning on the Marino systems before. What kind of information would you be looking for?"

"Anything that might reflect poorly on him. Questionable finances. Correspondence that points to secrets. Anything and everything."

"You were quite careful to keep most things out

of your emails. I couldn't put your plan together simply from your digital footprint. Dante has been just as careful."

"Perhaps. But it doesn't hurt to look again, does it? Especially if you can go back into the past, when his security might have been more lacking, or he understood less about computers and the like."

Saverina considered this. "I couldn't do it on company time. Or at my home. It can't connect to Parisi."

"I know it is one of your little rules, but my apartment is the best option. We are portraying an engaged couple. Why shouldn't you spend time there?"

She frowned and said nothing—clearly understanding it was the best option and clearly not wanting to give in. "It would not be wise. You were right last night. There's chemistry between us, but I won't be engaging in it any longer. Best we keep our space."

He sighed, finally realizing he'd never understand this stand of hers. "I simply don't understand, Saverina. Why must things change? We can enjoy each other's company—in and outside of the bedroom. Accomplish all our goals and revenges. We get along, and we are attracted to each other. Perhaps the relationship isn't 'real' in any romantic way, but is working toward a common goal and enjoying each other not better than most romantic relationships that end in heartbreak and anger and theatrics?"

He was sure these words would change her mind. She had always behaved as a rational, sensible woman. Instead, she took a long sip of water, then leaned forward and fixed him with a hard glare. "Have you ever been in a romantic relationship, Teo?"

He did not have a quick response for that. He'd never had any desire to complicate the enjoyable pursuit of sex with the trap of feelings. So, *no*, but he also hesitated to give her ammunition for whatever onslaught she was currently planning. "Probably not by *your* definition."

She rolled her eyes. "All right then. Did you love your mother?"

He cooled considerably at the mention of his mother. He'd told Saverina a bit about her, but mostly just that she'd suffered a long disease and then passed. "I cannot fathom what my mother has to do with any of this."

"Clearly she factors into your revenge. You're doing this because Dante refused to acknowledge you, but that has to connect to your mother. The question is, did you love her?"

He leaned back in his chair, resisting the urge to get up and leave. But retreating just because she poked at a wound wouldn't get him what he wanted. Which was things back to the way they were on his road to revenge. "Are there people who don't love their mothers?"

She let out an odd sigh. One that made him want to reach out, skim a hand over her hair. The part of him that wanted to break her rules earlier was quite glad they were in place now.

"Toward the end of my mother's life, I'm not sure what I felt for her," Saverina said softly. Then she let out a bitter kind of laugh. "I've never told anyone that. Not even my therapist. I guess enemy-friends are good for something after all."

"We are not enemies, *bedda*."

She ignored that. "You asked me about romantic relationships. Before I can answer, I need to understand something. The point of my question is, have you ever loved anyone?"

"That is not *my* point."

"Humor me, then, Teo. Tell me about how you grew up. The normal things engaged people might know about each other."

"You mean the things you did not know when you agreed to marry me?"

She looked at him for a long second that made him want to do the unthinkable. Shift in his seat. "Perhaps I should just go."

He wanted to be unaffected enough to invite her to do just that. But his *plan*. He needed people seeing them together. That was the only reason he considered her request. The only reason he began to speak of a time he did not care to remember.

"Our lives were very isolated. Mamma was afraid of retribution from Dante. So she steered clear of her family, lest they get involved. She stayed here in Palermo. She cleaned offices in a large building, and I worked alongside her."

"What about school?"

"She educated me as a young child. When it became clear I wanted to go to university, she put me in public school. I was old enough to be focused on my studies by then. The only thing I was concerned with was doing what I could to create the potential to save my mother from her concerns. I did not make friends. I did not *date*, if that is what you're asking. I had only one goal. To keep her safe."

"And then she died anyway."

It hit like the slice of a knife. Sharp and so cold he could scarcely manage an easy breath. "How kind of you to point that out," he returned, his words utterly devoid of any inflection.

"Both of my parents were dead by the time I was eleven," she said. "I didn't have a great relationship with either of them, and still, it's world-altering when a parent dies."

"Perhaps. But I was not a girl of eleven. I was a man of thirty."

She lifted her elegant shoulders. "I don't think it matters, Teo."

It mattered. Because her death had given him a new purpose. A name for his nameless father. All the revenge he needed.

"While you were lying to me—"

"I was not—"

"You were lying to me," she cut him off sharply. "You led me to believe you loved me and wanted to spend your life with me."

"I don't recall ever using those words."

She inhaled sharply—and made him wish he hadn't said that.

"No, you didn't." She shook her head. "The point of all this, the reason it can't just *go back*, is because a real relationship is based on trust and respect and love. It ends poorly—with those theatrics you mentioned—when one of those things are broken. You want me to forgo the pursuit of love, trust, and respect in order to protect myself from those things being broken. I think I even understand why you'd feel you must avoid those things. For me? I can't simply…decide I don't want those things. Protect and insulate myself from those things because they might *hurt* in the end."

He did not care for the word *avoid*. It painted him as a coward when what he prided himself on being was *rational*.

"I will never trust you, Teo. Not now. So there is no hope that this turns into what *I* want. I can't go back. We can only move forward with our mutual goal and my carefully considered ground rules." She pulled a paper from her purse—the ridiculous *ground* rules she'd written out in her pretty, precise handwriting. She pushed it across the table to him. "If you cannot agree to all of these, I cannot agree to be part of your revenge."

Teo ran his tongue over his teeth in an effort to remind himself to be as rational as he prided himself on being. Irritation with her—with the *loss* of her—was pointless. Because revenge was all that mattered.

"Very well," he said when he trusted himself to speak calmly. "Then you will have to follow a few of *mine*." He pulled a pen from his pocket, flipped her paper over, and began to write.

CHAPTER EIGHT

SAVERINA FROWNED AS Teo wrote. *His* ground rules.

As if he had *any* right.

She considered leaving again. She did not *have* to do this. Lorenzo had told her for years he didn't need Dante to pay, so maybe she shouldn't want that either. Maybe she should leave this for Teo. Perhaps Dante had spent years dragging Lorenzo's name through the mud, but that was not nearly as awful as refusing to acknowledge your son. Creating an environment where the mother of your child lived in fear in isolation.

But she couldn't let the idea of revenge go. Not just for Lorenzo anymore. For a little boy who'd been raised the way Teo had outlined. Saverina was well-versed in sad and bad childhoods. They came in all shapes and sizes, and she could never be immune to feeling compassion for those who found ways to succeed in spite of their upbringing.

And more… Oh, she hated herself for it, but Teo's story of his childhood had softened her. Not enough to change her rules, of course. Just enough that it was hard to hate him. That she thought…he wasn't so much hard and cold and mean.

He was misguided. He didn't understand love. He'd only known it from his mother, and no doubt her death had made it feel like more weapon than joy. Saverina might have felt that too…if she had not had her siblings. If Lorenzo had not found Brianna. If she had not watched love and family change him.

She blew out a breath, knowing this was a dangerous line of thought. She could feel sympathy for him, she could work with him, but she could not under any circumstances believe she could *change* him. That she could teach him how to love.

Right?

Teo handed her his list of rules, and she tried to shake her traitorous thoughts away. She took the paper and skimmed over the harsh ink strokes, trying to use this ridiculous farce as enough of an insult to harden her foolish heart to him.

Any information gathered on Dante Marino will be immediately shared with me.

Well, she didn't really care so much about that. As far as she saw it, they needed each other to create the worst-case scenario for Dante.

We will attend any and all events I see fit.

She tried not to scowl. He did not get to dictate when she went *anywhere*.

I will have wardrobe approval at such events.

She nearly laughed out loud, though she kept it in. Clearly he was trying to make her mad.

We will eat lunch together every workday from now on.

Smart, but she didn't like it. Spending all this time together? No, she didn't think that was wise at all.

I will drive you home from work every day—except on evenings we attend an event together.

Over her dead body.

It was an utterly absurd list, but when she looked at his self-satisfied expression, she knew it was on purpose. He thought her rules were silly, so he would make a few silly rules of his own. He probably thought she would explode over the wardrobe approval at the very least.

Well, she wasn't going down without a fight, but it would be the fight *she* chose. Not the one he expected. She slid the rules back to him. "Teo, this is ridiculous."

"Why?" he asked, too much innocence in his expression for anyone with a brain to believe.

"We don't need to be in each other's pockets for people to believe we're engaged. The only person we have to fool is Dante Marino."

"All of this will aid in our efforts to do exactly that—because for Dante to believe it, the media must believe it and report upon it. They must be interested enough to take our picture, to dig around. Now, if you will not come to my apartment, if you will not allow *touch*, then I'm afraid time is what you must give me to accomplish my goal." He paused. "*Our* goal," he amended.

But she didn't believe he really saw it as *our*. He

saw her as a tool. Maybe it hurt a little, but she didn't have to be the tool he wanted. She could be the tool she chose. Right now, she chose to be calm and rational. "Driving me home breaks *my* rule of us being alone together. You'll have to cross that one out."

"Then I refuse your no touching rule."

She didn't react immediately. She made sure her expression was stoic. Throwing a fit or getting angry only seemed to play into his hand. She had to be as calm and collected as he was. As much of a strategic game player as he was.

When she spoke, her voice was cool and breezy. She hoped. "Why should you want to touch me, Teo? Surely you can slake your manly lust elsewhere." The thought made her want to *die*, but she'd never, ever let him know that.

"Not as long as we are engaged, *bedda*." He reached out, took her hand. The one with the fake engagement ring on her pointer finger. So much faking. So much pretending.

She wished the heat that seeped into her at his touch was either of those things. That her heart wouldn't soar at the idea he might be faithful to her when all he was being faithful to was his revenge.

"You have my word," he said, pulling her hand to his mouth. Pressing a kiss to the top of her hand.

For *show*.

She hated it. *Hated* the way it made her want his mouth on hers. *Hated* how it made her feel young and vulnerable and insipid—such a little fool who'd be fooled by him once then still allow attraction to cloud her thinking. Who—despite knowing better in a million different ways, many that had played out before her in the hovel she'd grown up in—thought she might be able to *change* him.

Wasn't that her mother's fatal flaw? Believing that her father would change? Would suddenly love her?

Saverina refused to let someone have that kind of control over *her*. Never. Ever. If she ever fell in love again—if she ever married—it would be for *real* love. The kind that was reciprocated. The kind you didn't have to fight for.

Control. In this moment she had to find some. "Very well. I will amend my no touching rule. You may engage in public displays if necessary." She withdrew her hand from his with a little jerk against his grip. "On the condition you will cross off driving me home every night. If we arrive at events together, we will use a driver."

"Whatever you say, *principessa*."

She wouldn't bristle at the way he said that. Wouldn't think about the way he'd used that term when proposing. *Fake* proposing.

"Any other quibbles?" he asked, again with the feigned innocence.

"Not at present." She even managed to smile.

If he was taken off guard, it was only a flash of a second before he settled into a distantly amused expression she refused to let affect her. "I have to admit, I expected you to have something to say about the wardrobe approval."

She smiled over at him with all the fake sweetness she could muster. "But I've lived all my life for a man to tell me how to dress for an event." She batted her eyelashes at him. Because she knew the first event—the gala—she'd wear something that would make him regret such an attempt at control.

Teo did not appreciate being ordered about. He could not fathom why he was following Saverina's instructions to the letter.

It is all for the end result. Revenge.

Right. He straightened his jacket and walked to Saverina's front door. He'd texted her, per her instructions. *Imagine.* It was the modern version of honking at a woman's door and hoping she emerged.

The driver of his car stood at the passenger door, ready to open it for them. Another one of Saverina's demands. Couldn't be alone, even for a second.

Ridiculous. The whole thing was ridiculous, and maybe he was playing along because he needed her for the severest form of revenge, but that did not mean he had to be a *lapdog*. She wanted to believe she had something over him, that she had some power here.

She did not. This was *his* revenge. *His* plan. He would do it his way, and if he made any accommodations along the way, it was because he wasn't a monster. He could be *quite* charitable. Always better to bend a little than break something.

Breaking things was the purview of Dante Marino, and Teo would not be like his biological father.

He had been raised by Giuseppa LaRosa. He would always do her kindness and sense of fair play justice.

Fair play did not mean bowing and scraping to Saverina like she was in charge. It meant *compromise*. So he did not storm into her home. He did not bang down the door. But he also did not wait by the car as instructed.

He moved to wait by the door. Technically not alone, because the driver stood in view. But he would not be able to hear anything said should Teo and Saverina have a conversation before walking down to the drive.

He meandered up the walk, enjoying the gardens in the moonlight. The scent of flowers was earthy and exotic. The cool night settling in over the heat of the day a nice contrast. It was a pretty place. The kind of home he envisioned for himself once he and Saverina were married.

Because she would marry him, and she would play the dutiful wife. A Parisi-LaRosa union that would be a constant reminder to Dante and anyone who supported him that *Dante* lost at everything. Even revenge.

He heard the telltale creak of a door opening and turned to watch Saverina emerge. She stepped onto the little porch full of potted plants and flowers. The outdoor lights landed on her like a spotlight, and that's exactly where she should be. Looking like *that*.

She turned to lock her door, not yet seeing him there just a few yards away down the walk. When she was done and faced him once more, she came up a little short as their eyes clashed.

He could hardly think beyond the sudden fire in his body.

The outfit she wore was a bright, violent red. The top did not connect to the bottom. It was just a band around her generous breasts, baring her entire midriff. The skirt was long and flowing, but the slit in the fabric went dangerously high on her thigh.

He could not think past the onslaught of memory. The way she tasted. The way she felt when she came apart around him. He enjoyed sex—who wouldn't? But it had never become an insatiable hunger until *her*.

A thought that didn't do to dwell on.

She kept her distance, but she smiled at him now. "Does this dress meet with your approval?" She pretended to look at her watch. "We have time for me to go in and change should it not."

"Dress?" He laughed, irritated at how raw that laugh sounded. "That is hardly a dress."

She rolled her eyes. "It is high-fashion, Teo. Would you rather I dress like a nun?"

"I'm sure you'll be the talk of the gala," he managed to say, despite the raging of his own body. Moonlight dappled her dark hair. Her eyes seemed to shine, an otherworldly glow out here among the flowers and stars.

He wanted his hands on her so badly he had to curl his fingers into a fist. Fight back the cloudy haze of lust and want like he was doing real physical battle.

"That's what we intend, is it not? People to talk, wonder, and poke into things?" She fished around in her little purse.

"It is exactly what we intend."

She looked up at him, her eyebrows furrowed. "And yet, you seem…tense. Is everything all right?"

It was *not* a genuine question. She was playing a very dangerous game, and he had two choices. Call her out on it.

Or play along.

He moved closer to her now and watched the wariness creep into her eyes. But she did not back away. Did not hold him off. Even as he stepped up onto the porch with her.

She angled that beautiful face up, all regal condescension. "Then we should be on our way."

He looked down at her, let his gaze take in the elegant curve of her neck, the enticing line of her shoulder. The way that little strip of fabric held her breasts in place and on display. Particularly when she inhaled a little more sharply than she had been. Because heat arced between them, raw and potent. An electricity he did not understand why she was so intent on denying. All over something as pointless and unpredictable as *love*.

Her perfume wafted around him. Something spicy and sultry and intoxicating. When his eyes finished their tour of her body, he met her dark gaze. Warm and needy. Pink stained her cheeks—not from the elaborate makeup she wore, but from *desire*.

"You want me, Saverina," he murmured. Still not

touching her, no matter how much his body demand he did just that. "Why deny it?"

She let out a careful breath. It didn't shake, but he could tell that was hard won.

"It's not *wanting* you on a sexual level, since heaven knows that's all you mean, that I deny, Teo," she said, clearly if a little breathlessly. "It's allowing a liar to have access to my body that I deny. You can trust that is not much of a punishment on *my* end."

She was an excellent liar, but he knew she lied. Because she could hate him for his subterfuge. She could spend the rest of her life not trusting him. But she knew and felt as well as he did what they could create together. And denying it was a physical pain, even if a necessary one.

"Trust, *bedda*, I know just how much pleasure I offered you. You can pretend you don't miss it, if that makes you feel better." Then he stepped off the porch and held out his arm for her. "Now, we have places to be. Let us not be late."

CHAPTER NINE

SAVERINA REFUSED TO consider the dress a mistake. She'd been waiting for an appropriate place to wear it, and this gala was just such an event. Yes, she'd hoped that the way she looked in it might *punish* Teo, and she liked to think it had. She'd seen the flare of desire in his eyes. She knew he *wanted* her, in a physical way, if nothing else.

She just hadn't thought about the fact that it would punish *her* as well. Because the way he looked at her—not just outside her home, but here at the gala— made her wish it was his hands not his gaze on every last inch of her.

She did not understand how she could be so hurt by someone and still *want* them. She was beginning to realize she'd still had a child's black-and-white outlook on life. Now she had to adjust to something more…complicated. Gray areas and moral complications.

She hated it.

Still, she smiled. She chatted. She didn't stick to Teo's side or vice versa, but they had arrived together, and at strategic points throughout the night they shared a chat, got a drink from the bar together, cozied up with each other in a corner.

Saverina could feel the interest from some people—mostly the people she worked with. The way eyes followed them when they were together, when they drifted apart.

She would have to call Lorenzo tonight as most of those people were his employees and would no doubt find a way to pass along what they'd seen the minute Lorenzo returned if not sooner. She supposed she could tell her brother the truth about pretending with Teo to get revenge—without the little bit about how Teo had fooled her for so long—but he'd no doubt tell her to stand down. Not important or too dangerous or *whatever*.

No, she would have to lie to her brother. Pretend she was desperately in love with Teo. She glanced across the large ballroom, her eyes landing on his tall, impressive frame. He spoke with two other Parisi executives, but she didn't even notice who. Because her heart twisted in her chest.

It wasn't a lie that she loved him, no matter how she wished it was. The lie would be that he loved her back. She blew out a breath and took a sip of her champagne. She should drift closer, give Teo a reason to break off from his business associates, but she liked her little corner where no one really noticed her. Where she could *breathe* and fortify herself against the next Teo attack.

You want me.

The dark way he'd said that there in the pretty evening in one of her favorite places. Looking so handsome it hurt. If she would have left her answer at *yes*, opened her door, they'd be back in her room rather than here.

And that would have been a mistake, she reminded herself harshly.

Maybe she'd enjoy the moment of being with him again—okay, no maybes. She *would* enjoy it. Until it was over. Then she would have all the same hurts, and even more regrets.

She didn't want that.

Suddenly Teo was at her elbow. He leaned close. "Dante is here," he murmured.

She scanned the crowd. Dante was over by the bar talking to a few men.

"Did you know he would be here?" Saverina asked.

"No. He was not on the guest list." There was a grimness to Teo's expression that Saverina didn't think would do well for the overall plan. She slid her hand up to his shoulder and tried to harden herself against any reaction.

"Come, let's dance," she suggested. When he raised an eyebrow at her, she shrugged. "You can't spend the rest of the gala glaring at him or people will talk in a way you do not want. Yet. Come." This time she took his arm and tugged him forward to the dance floor, where a nice slow song was playing.

He did not precisely wipe the glare off his face, but when he pulled her into his arms for a dance, some of that grimness faded. And then they danced. Easily and in time, like they were perfectly matched to do just this.

Part of her wanted to lean her head against his chest and just…give in. Allow his pretend. She could love him and he could not love her and would it really be so bad?

She thought of her mother toward the end of her life. Ragged, used, lost. All because she'd loved a man who wouldn't love her back. Saverina didn't think she was *that* weak. She could go into this knowing Teo's limitations.

Then again, the hope of his someday understanding love might eventually kill her.

"Perhaps we should make an early exit," she said, because it turned out pretending to be who she wanted to be on the outside, while knowing she couldn't be on the inside, was *exhausting*. And Teo kept looking at Dante when he should ignore the man all together.

"To be chased away by *him*?"

"So people might talk about *why* we left early and together after slow dancing, Teo." She looked up at him, trying to get through that vibrating anger. "Your plan, remember?"

The plan. Never before had Teo wanted to damn the plan. Stride across the room and strike the man. *This* was why he steered clear of spaces Dante was in. His fury overrode all attempts at control. Being in proximity to the man who'd harmed his mother, who'd threatened to crush him if he revealed his parentage always threatened to undermine the plan in a blatant explosion.

If Teo thought that would be satisfying in the long run, he'd give in to it. But Dante would twist it. Teo would likely end up in jail for assault, and Teo would never have his revenge.

So, yes, the plan was essential. "Very well," he muttered. "We will make a hasty exit. Keep your hand in mine."

He half expected her to argue, but she'd been surprisingly obedient—a word she'd no doubt hate to be used on her—this evening. She smiled, she touched, she danced. It was an act. He could see that by the shadows that lingered in her eyes. But it was a *good* act. Only someone who knew her would notice those shadows.

He did not interrogate why *he* did.

They left the dance floor hand in hand, and Teo headed for the door, but he made a *slight* detour. He steered Saverina right toward Dante. Not for a confrontation, no. In fact, he turned his head away from Dante and pretended to nod at a colleague on the opposite side of the room as he moved Saverina farther toward the door.

"Is he looking?" Teo asked under his breath.

"Oh, yes."

"Good." It was *good*. Dante had to know who Saverina was by sight, and if he did not, surely someone would inform him. From there, Dante would begin to wonder. He would begin to worry. The son he wanted to crush. The sister of the business rival he hated. If Dante did not start seeing him as a threat now, he would be a stupid man.

Teo thought many unflattering things about Dante Marino, but he did not think the man stupid.

Teo escorted Saverina to their waiting limo. Once inside, she watched the city pass by as the vehicle headed for her house. Teo was too lost in his own plans and machinations to worry about conversation, but about halfway through the drive, she turned to him.

"When did you find out about Dante possibly being your father?"

Since it brought back unwanted memories of his mother's deathbed, he hedged. "Why do you ask me this?"

"Humor me."

He did not *need* to humor her, but he found himself giving in anyway. "Almost two years ago. Mamma informed me of my biological father's name with her last breath." He could have left that detail out. He did not want her pity, but he also wanted her to understand that his revenge would always come first.

For his mother.

She was quiet for a long moment. He could see her only in the way lights flashed through the window as they passed other cars and streetlights. He knew she looked at him, and he was more than happy to find himself mostly shrouded in the dark.

"How did you find out the rest, then?" she asked

quietly. "About him threatening her, and what you told me the other night?"

"Careful research and study. Putting together stories from speaking to her family, from what I dug up on Dante, and so forth. I tracked down an old employee of the Marino household who had known my mother, and she filled in the remaining gaps. She had no love lost for Dante."

Another silence stretched out between them, and he assumed that would be that. Assumed it so much he refused to say anything else. He would not tell her what the past two years had been like.

But he *wanted* to. All those words on the tip of his tongue. It was a twisted desire in him. So Saverina would see. So she would understand.

He did not need any of these things from her, no matter what his traitorous heart whispered. All he needed from her was what they'd agreed upon.

When she spoke again, her tone was still quiet, careful. He did not like how close it sounded to *pity.*

"You say *her* family, but if they were hers, they are yours too."

Teo shook his head before he realized she couldn't see him. "They did not know I existed. They live in northern Italy. To them, my mother was long dead before she died—and I inconsequential."

"Are you sure about that?"

Since he was not—he had not left any possibility for some silly reunion. Why should they care for him or about him? Too many years passed, too much… *Dante* in him. He'd felt they'd be happier not knowing he existed. "When I spoke to them, I did not mention who I was or what exactly I was after. They do not know my mother had a son. They did not need to."

"But—"

"No buts, Saverina. This is not a fairy tale." He refused to believe in such things. "For thirty years they did not know of my existence. They thought my mother simply turned away from them. Best for everyone if that does not change. That is the end of this discussion."

"You don't think they'd want to know their family *didn't* turn away from them? That they have more family? A piece of her?"

A piece of her. That twisted inside of him like shrapnel. But she was no longer here. There were no pieces left. "That is the end of this discussion, Saverina," he growled.

There was a considering silence, and he thought she'd let it go. Thought she'd *listen*. He should have known better.

"It's painful for you," she said softly. She even reached out and touched his arm. Initiating touch even though it was against her rules. This was not public because the driver was separated from them by the screen. This touch was not an act.

He blamed his surprise over that for not stopping her before she said the rest.

"But pain is not such a bad thing, Teo. Dealing with your pain and grief often leads to beautiful things on the other side."

There was no other side of the loss of his mother. There was only revenge. He pulled his arm away from her touch. "I do not know what this is, Saverina, but I will never give you what you want."

She inhaled sharply, jerked her hand back, and scooted into her little corner where he couldn't see her expression even in the passing lights. "I feel sorry for you, Teo," she murmured, her voice icy now.

"You should not. I soon will have everything I've ever wanted."

"No, you won't. You will get your revenge, *we* will get our revenge, but then your whole life will stretch out in front of you, and then what?"

"I will enjoy it."

She laughed. Bitterly. "You wouldn't know how. You isolate yourself from anything and everything that might be *enjoyable*. You refuse to look at all the hurts you've been dealt. You think pushing them away will make them go away, but trust me, they won't. The hurts linger until you deal with them."

It was his turn for a bitter laugh. "You'll have to excuse me, *principessa*, if I do not take a pampered heiress's word on *hurts* and *grief*."

He thought that harshness would shut her up. Perhaps he was even desperate for it to.

"That might hurt my feelings if it were true, Teo. But you know my story. You know it has not all been pampering and easy. Which leads me to believe you're nothing more than a lion with a thorn in its paw. Roaring and lashing out because of your *own* pain."

"I haven't begun to roar and lash out, *bedda.*"

She only made a considering sound, and they spent the rest of the drive in silence. But he could not fully erase her words, her experience from his mind. And *that* was unforgiveable.

CHAPTER TEN

SAVERINA COULD HAVE kept arguing with him, but he would only build walls there. Where it hurt and he didn't even *realize* it. So blinded by his revenge—by this thing that he thought took the grief away.

But the grief never went away. Whether you loved a parent or not. There was always grief—whether they were gone or whether they'd never been what they should have been. She wished this understanding would help harden her heart to him, but all it did was soften it.

He was a grown man with the world at his fingertips, and she'd been a young, confused girl working through her grief. But the real difference between them was even in the absence of her parents—both when they'd been alive and after they'd died, after Rocca had died—she'd had her family. Not just Lorenzo, but all her many brothers and sisters who'd looked after one another, made sure they were all okay.

Teo had *no one*.

But pushing at him would make it impossible to

ever get that through to him. Maybe it was a pipe dream to think if she was careful, she might be able to help him. The way she and her siblings had once helped Lorenzo realize that loving Brianna was a gift—not a punishment.

But sometimes a woman had to believe in a pipe dream to get through the day. As long as she didn't pin *everything* on him reciprocating, she would not end up like her mother. She tried to assure herself of this.

The car pulled to a stop in front of her private entrance to the sprawling Parisi estate. She should immediately say her goodbyes and get out, but… There had been something she'd wanted to broach with him before they'd gotten on the subject of his lost family.

She glanced at the partition between them and driver. No doubt soundproof, but she couldn't be too careful with this.

"Come inside. I'll have someone bring us a nightcap."

"A nightcap." She couldn't see him in the dark, but she could feel the sarcasm of a raised eyebrow all the same.

"It's not *that* kind of invitation, Teo," she said on a sigh. "We have something to discuss."

She got out of the car when the driver opened her door. She offered him a smile, then strode for her entrance without looking back to see if Teo had followed.

Of course he followed.

She swept inside, smiled at Antonina. "Could you fix up a tray for us? Bring it into my parlor?"

Antonina nodded and disappeared to do as she was asked. Saverina kept walking through the hall, refusing to look back at Teo. She wasn't breaking her own rule. She was bending it. For business. Besides, any number of staff people were about... They weren't *alone* alone as long as they stayed in her parlor.

She led him into said room, a wide-open affair full of plants and windows and no privacy whatsoever. It was as close to a greenhouse as she could get inside the house. The plants were something that steadied her when she was feeling precarious. She loved this room, and while she didn't really want memories of Teo in here, it was the right room for her purposes.

She trusted Lorenzo's staff with everything, even secrets. They might *mention* Teo's attendance here, but they would not listen in on the conversation. They would not act as *spies*.

She settled herself on the little settee. She finally steeled herself enough to look at Teo and smile. "You may sit there," she said regally, pointing to the same settee she was on—but the opposite side.

His expression was one of bemusement, and he said nothing as he sat himself where she pointed. Of course he was so tall, the spread of his legs meant there was very little space between them.

This could not matter. She kept the pleasant smile on her face as Antonina entered with a tray of the little sweets Saverina preferred, along with a small collection of expensive alcohol bottles and glasses.

"Would you like me to pour?" Antonina asked.

Saverina waved her away. "Thank you. I'll handle it."

The woman nodded and then left them alone. Saverina fixed Teo a drink to the exact specifications she wished she didn't know, but there were more important things to discuss than her feelings. Or his.

So she got right down to it. She handed him a drink, didn't bother with one for herself.

"Did you ever hear about the attack on Dante's oldest son about five years ago?"

"Yes, I read about it. They never found who did it, but Dante tried to blame your brother."

Saverina nodded, angry all over again even though the accusation had never truly stuck to Lorenzo, no matter how Dante had tried. It *had* hurt Lorenzo's reputation at the time, though. He'd been painted as a violent monster. And he'd *let* people paint him that way.

She'd never understood how Lorenzo could just… accept that. Step into that. He'd been right in the end. Eventually the rumors had ceased. Nothing had come from it.

But even the memory of what the papers and gossip sites and such had said about her brother made her angry.

"Yes. Not the first time he tried to pin something on Lorenzo, but possibly the most successful at the time for swaying public opinion. Lorenzo lost a few clients, but he didn't fight back. He knew it wasn't true, so he didn't see the point in fighting Dante at his own game."

"Pity."

Saverina laughed. She couldn't help it. It *was* a pity.

"Dante's pattern for blaming your brother for the bad things that happened to him or his business is why I targeted getting a position at Parisi. Clearly he has a vendetta against your brother. Do you know why?"

Saverina sighed. "No. Lorenzo has always maintained he has never understood a reason other than the fact that Parisi was a business rival that wouldn't be crushed like the rest. Dante is a textbook narcissist who can't stand the fact he once lost a client to my brother. Of course, these days Lorenzo says it's simply because he has everything Dante wants."

"What's that?"

Teo would not care for the answer, but Saverina considered it more deeply than she ever had. "Happiness," she said gently. She'd thought that was Lorenzo being blinded by love talking, but now…

She just wondered if it were true. Could happiness and not worrying about revenge and competition really be the answer?

Teo's scowl told her, *Not with this man*.

Happiness. Teo grunted irritably. *Happiness*. A man like Dante wouldn't know what to do with happiness if it landed in his lap, so how could he be jealous of it in Lorenzo?

Teo glanced at Saverina. Dangerously close on the fussy little sofa. The smell of her perfume seemed to wrap around him, as it had done on the dance floor. The memory of her in his arms as they danced tonight was too potent.

Happiness.

Would *he* know what to do with it?

Well, he'd find out when he got his revenge. Because it was the only thing that could bring true happiness. That couldn't shatter and break. That couldn't leave a hole so big and wide it hardly mattered the good that had come from it.

People died. Revenge didn't.

"I had just started university at the time," Saverina continued, clearly focused on something he couldn't quite follow yet. "Furious someone would print such blatant lies about my brother, obviously. Lorenzo was also angry, I could tell, but he wanted to keep me out of it."

"I'm sure you took that equitably," Teo muttered. He knew her too well. She would not have taken that easily.

She laughed, and Teo found himself leaning toward that sound. He missed her laugh. Her genuine smiles. He missed…

Well, nothing he wouldn't have again. She'd get over this foolish, naive need for love. They'd have what they had before, and everything would be quite simple and easy. He was sure of it.

He always got what he wanted these days.

"I know he was worried *I* would become a target if I waded in. Lorenzo knew Dante could be ruthless even if the public didn't. I understood his reticence to let me in. He's always taken my protection quite seriously."

For a strange moment, Teo felt…arrested. Deep within. The idea that Saverina being in Dante's orbit might make her a target… He closed his hands into fists. He would kill first. But this was ridiculous, as he wasn't putting her in any danger at all.

"But no, I did not take his warning me off well. I was determined to get to the bottom of the perpetrator of the attack. I'd already been developing my computer skills at that point, so I used them. To determine the police's suspects, to track where Dante was getting his information."

"They never even found a suspect for the attack."

"No, but with what I did gather, I developed a… theory. I've never been able to prove it. It's totally a theory of my own making based on circumstance, but perhaps it's a theory we should consider once again."

He knew he should focus on her story—it might lead him to an even stronger thread of revenge. Leverage. Everything he wanted. But all he could focus on was the part of her background that didn't make sense.

"Whyever don't you work in the Parisi IT department, Saverina?"

This question clearly surprised her. She made an

odd little noise, then lifted her hand to flutter it in a strange gesture he'd never seen her use before. Almost as if she was flustered. Over a rather straightforward and easy question, all in all.

"It doesn't matter," she insisted. "What matters is, though I couldn't prove my theory at the time and I let it go since I couldn't, his wife stopped attending events with him after the attack on their son. Dante only ever comes to these sorts of things alone now, but before the attack on their son, she was always at his side, or she and his boys. They were always the picture-perfect family. The perfect contrast to Lorenzo's singlehood and complicated background before Brianna."

"The reports are that she suffers from some kind of condition." Though Teo had never spent much time digging into Dante's wife. She'd seemed rather inconsequential, especially since she did not attend events with the man anymore. The former staff member who'd once filled him in on what had happened to his mother had only sung Mrs. Marino's praises.

"This very well could be, but I've always wondered. Could Dante have ordered the attack on his son himself? Could he have *done* it himself? Could his wife have found out about it? Is *that* why she stopped attending events right after the attack and has continued all these years? Is *that* why no perpetrator was ever found?"

Teo could only stare at her, sitting elegantly on her elaborate sofa, that excuse for a dress making her skin seem to glow gold. It would have threatened to be a distraction if the bomb she dropped was not quite so big.

Could Dante have attacked his own son? And for what? Just to blame Lorenzo? It was cruel and insane, but Teo was not above believing those things of Dante. And if it was true…

He reached out, all her rules be damned, and took her hand. Squeezed. "We must prove it, Saverina. *You* must prove it."

She swallowed and looked away. "I will see what I can do, of course, but if I couldn't find proof when it happened, how could I find proof now? Maybe you should hire someone else. Someone with real experience in investigation."

She sounded oddly…insecure, when she'd always been so sure of herself. She was a confident woman, and she'd stood up to him time and again. Hell, she'd hacked into all his systems, followed him to that bar. Why should she seem…fragile now?

"It was years ago when you tried. You were a *teenager*. You're older, wiser. No doubt you have access to better equipment. You can do this. You will do this."

She shook her head and withdrew her hand from his, lurching to her feet. "N-no. That's…not the deal." Her breathing was coming in little pants, the words sounding a bit strangled. He stood too, reaching out for her without fully understanding why. Just the instinctive need to calm her.

But she stumbled backward, only keeping herself upright by pressing against the wall. Her eyes were wide. She was gasping like a drowning person. Panic radiated off of her in waves.

"Saverina," he said, careful to keep his voice even although her panic sliced through him. But demanding to know what was happening certainly wouldn't calm her. "*Bedda*, breathe."

"Can't," she gasped. Her gaze was wild.

"Yes," he returned as he stepped closer. "You can. You are fine and well and safe. Come, Saverina. Hold on to me." He held out his hand, heart hammering in his chest. He knew he could not simply grab her. It could cause whatever panic was hurting her to expand.

She had to make the choice. For long, terrible moments she just stood there, struggling to breathe and staring at him with wide eyes. Then slowly, very slowly, she reached a trembling hand toward his outstretched one.

He grasped it quickly, then didn't bother with the rest. He swept her up in his arms. She shouldn't be on her feet anymore. "Come, *bedda*. We will sit, and all will be well," he murmured with more certainty than he felt.

He carried her to the little couch, kept her safe in his lap as she shook and gasped for air. He could not give her air, and that about cut him in two. But she held on to him, trembling and struggling.

The only other time he'd ever felt so helpless was watching his mother fade away. The memory should have filled him with anger anew, but he couldn't get there past all his worry for Saverina.

When she finally began to settle, he skimmed a hand over her hair, setting it back to rights. "Explain this?"

"N-nothing." Her shoulders slumped, and she leaned into him. He held her close. It wasn't nothing. That much was clear. But he didn't prod her, just held her until she was breathing normally again.

CHAPTER ELEVEN

WHEN THE WORST of the attack was over, Saverina was too exhausted and wrung out to even feel embarrassment. Yet. It would come, but not tonight.

All in all, it wasn't the worst one she'd ever had, though it had come on more quickly than they usually did. Usually she had time to remove herself, time to access her coping skills. This one had hit hard and fast and with no warning.

The way he'd grasped her hand, so certain, so impassioned. *"You will do this."* It had just set off an immediate panic inside her, because she had *tried* to prove this once before and failed. No one had known, so while it had been frustrating, it hadn't been a failure.

Now it would be. The panic threatened to curl around her once more, so she simply breathed in the spicy scent of Teo's cologne and enjoyed—when she absolutely should not—the feeling of utter safety in his arms.

It was embarrassing but not terrible. She'd rather have an attack in front of Teo than have one in public or in front of her family. She did not have to worry about Teo blaming himself for her own issues like she did with all her siblings.

"Come. Explain," he said. He spoke gently, calmly, but it was a demand. She found this was one of the rare instances when a demand kind of worked rather than made her angry. It gave her a clear next step, helped her brain focus on the answer, not the panic still fluttering around inside of her.

"I…have panic attacks sometimes. An old vestige of a traumatic childhood. It is nothing to concern yourself over. I spent some years in therapy dealing with the worst of it." She wanted to get up off the settee, his *lap* for heaven's sake, but her legs were shaky. Every part of her was shaking.

"How have I never seen such a thing?" he asked, not in accusation, but with a kind of confusion. Still, he just held her against him like sitting curled up with each other was the most natural thing in the world.

It would *never* be, she reminded herself harshly, no matter how much she liked the feeling of being held and looked after. "It is rare that I have them these days. I have gotten help, and I know how to avoid my triggers, for the most part."

"Triggers. Such as?"

This question was enough to have her pushing against him. She couldn't stand just yet, but she managed to maneuver off his lap, out of his arms and to her own side of the settee. Discussing her triggers was *not* avoiding them.

"It is of no consequence." Did he really need to know all her weaknesses? He'd no doubt exploit them to his own ends.

"How can I avoid them for you if I do not know them?"

This seemed like a reasonable question, but they were not friends. He was not her real boyfriend or fiancé. He did not love her or care for her anyway. At best, he was attracted to her and didn't *hate* her. At the end of the day, he was just a man using her to aid in his revenge.

He'd made that very clear.

"Why would you care to avoid them, Teo?" She rubbed at her temples, where the usual after-attack headache was beginning to make itself known. She did not have the energy to guard herself against him. She had to find some way to finish their conversation and send him on his way.

He did not answer her for a long time. So long it felt like she *had* to look at him. Confusion was etched across his beautiful face. She doubted that was a very common feeling for him. "You are not my enemy, Saverina," he said, very seriously.

"You say that like it's a positive." And she could not go believing neutral statements were signs of love. She knew too well the path that led down.

"What triggered you this evening?" he pressed. Maybe confusion was rare, but giving up was rarer.

She was too tired to fight, so she simply gave in. "I don't like to fail."

"Who does?"

She shook her head. "I cannot explain it. The idea of certain failures…certain expectations…the pressure of it. I cannot handle it." She tried not to think of it as a weakness. Therapy had taught her that it was a natural result of a traumatic childhood. Not her fault, something to work through with no shame.

But sometimes it was impossible to leave shame behind no matter how aware she was that she *should*.

"This is why you do not work in the IT department? The pressure."

She could deny it, the logical leap he'd just made, but why bother? Maybe if he knew all her embarrassing little secrets, she'd stop being in love with him.

"Yes. I tend to put the most pressure on myself when it comes to my family. They…" She could not quite believe she was saying this, but why not lay it all out? It would never matter to him. It was freeing, almost. To say the things she'd only discussed with her university therapist out loud, to someone who was in her life. No matter how temporarily. "They sacrificed so much for me, particularly Lorenzo. I would never want them to know I struggle. With pressure, with anything. Lorenzo would blame himself."

"It seems who he would blame is his problem. Not yours."

"You don't have a family, Teo," she said. It was mean, she knew, but she thought it would get him to stop poking into her softest parts. "You cannot understand."

"Perhaps not. But the way other people blame

themselves—or don't—is hardly your responsibility. And Lorenzo dotes on you. He would not be hard on you in a position in the IT department."

She shook her head. "You don't understand," she repeated. Because no one ever did. "It's not about whether he would be hard on me. It's that I don't want him to be disappointed. I know I can be an excellent assistant—or whatever else I end up deciding to do at Parisi. A mistake as his assistant, in marketing or sales or whatever, would be embarrassing, but...inconsequential. A mistake in the IT department? It's the security of the entire company. He could lose everything. The consequences could be catastrophic. I couldn't..." The panic was closing in again. She breathed through it, focused on one of the hanging plants over by the window. The way the ivy twisted down toward the ground. Her little sanctuary where she was *safe*.

But there was a man here. A man she loved, who did not or would not love her back. And too many old hurts in the air around them.

"Very well," Teo murmured, as if he sensed she was on the edge of losing it again. "But you looking into Dante potentially being the one to attack his son is not pressure, *bedda*. We have a plan. Consider this...icing on the cake. If it does not come to fruition, it hardly matters."

But it did matter. She could see it in his eyes. He wanted this *so* badly, and she *shouldn't* feel obligated or pressured to give it to him. Not after what he'd done to her. But in a way that felt far too much like her childhood—her feelings and her rational thinking weren't meshing.

"You don't have to be kind, Teo. I know what it would mean to prove this."

He straightened out his jacket, brushed at lint that was most certainly not there, and *scoffed*. "No one has ever accused me of being kind."

But he was. Perhaps that was the heart of him. Behind all those walls and that need for revenge, he had a kind, bruised heart he'd rather harden than ever deal with. Hadn't she gone through that season in her life too?

She wished she were back in his lap. Wished she could just stay there in the circle of his arms where she'd felt protected and safe even as she struggled to breathe.

But she'd been protected her whole life. She'd spent university and the past year trying to prove to Lorenzo *and* herself that she could protect herself. That she could handle her life, her triggers, herself.

If only she could handle her heart. "I'll see what I can do."

Teo spent the next few days not allowing himself to consider Dante's possibly even larger downfall than he'd planned himself. He would not put that kind of pressure on Saverina. Every time he even considered the old story about Dante's son, he could only picture Saverina struggling to breathe.

So he tried not to think about it.

He did not consider the lack of pressure a kindness. He did not consider it anything but smart business. You did not ask something of someone that was more than they could handle. That would only ever end in disaster.

It was not *kindness*. It was sense.

He told himself this day after day, lunch after lunch, when he did not push her on the matter. Did not ask if she'd attempted to find anything regarding Dante's wife or son. He focused on his original plan. On how they would announce their engagement.

What he did *not* focus on was how much more he preferred these past few days *with* Saverina—no matter if she went home alone every night—than the one week he'd spent thinking she was off holidaying with her brother.

What he did *not* focus on was how every day at work, he looked more forward to his lunches with her, so much so that his work suffered in the mornings.

These things were frustrations, but they did not signify in the greater scheme of things. It was only good that he enjoyed the company of what was, essentially, a business partner. Revenge was a sort of business, after all. How nice they could share it.

But he would not grow to depend on this feeling. He would not tolerate it. His joy, his *happiness*—that thing foolish people put so much stock in—would only come from things he could control.

Never the fickle nature of *life*.

Or so he told himself. Even as he found himself wandering down toward Saverina's office a full fifteen minutes before her lunch break would begin. He convinced himself it was for the optics of it all. People would see him and gossip.

This was the goal.

Her office door was open when he approached. She stood with her back to the door, a phone cradled at her ear. She wore a silky shirt the color of sunrise and a skirt that skimmed the flare of her hips.

Something potent and raw slammed into his chest. Uncontrollable, but not as simple as lust. Lust was easy. But he knew now—having had her and knowing he wouldn't at the moment—that this lust lingered. Twisted. Sank into his bones until it felt like nights without her were torture.

Too close to grief to bear. *"The hurts linger until you deal with them."* She had said that to him, and those words, too, lingered in his head like a curse. Like she'd foisted *hurts* and *dealing* upon him when he knew *exactly* what he was about.

What he would do. What he wanted. But he wasn't above altering his plans when just cause presented itself. When this was over, maybe he would let her break off the engagement. She did deserve what *she* wanted, after all, and he had no interest in *love* and *families*.

Yes. That would be the new plan. The plan that would be *best*. Not because he was kind. Not because there were hurts not dealt with. But because... *Because*. He didn't need her. He did not need to force anyone to stay by his side.

He was Teo LaRosa, and he would *never* lower

himself to such things. So he would let her go because her staying would not give him what he wanted.

Peace and fulfillment in the wake of his revenge.

He wouldn't tell her that just yet, or maybe at all. He'd give her the illusion of it being her own decision later on. He would magnanimously agree. Let her go.

Be without her.

He scarcely realized his hands curled into fists.

When she turned, setting the phone down on the desk and lifting her gaze to see him there, her expression softened. He could not decide what it meant, but in a flash, her soft smile turned into that cool professionalism she wielded so well.

It felt like a punch to the gut. Like pain and hurt when it was just…business. The business of revenge and her finding out the truth. Which seemed like a better and better turn of events as days went on.

"I still have a few things to tie up before I can take my lunch break," she said, looking down at her desk rather than at him. "Perhaps I could meet you at the restaurant?"

Except that question felt as if it was posed to someone else. As if he was floating above this exchange, existing in a strange cloud of pain and a realization trying to break free.

He refused the realization, refused the feelings. He was Teo LaRosa, and he was in control of everything, and *everything* would lead him to destroying Dante Marino.

Saverina Parisi was *inconsequential*. Always.

She took a few steps toward him before she stopped

herself. She clutched her hands together. Her expression was cool, but he saw concern in her dark gaze. "Teo, are you all right?"

"Of course." Of course. He was always all right. He had a goal and he would meet it. What would ever *not* be all right about that? Maybe his throat felt tight and his words were raspy, but he was *excellent*.

Everything hinged on this goal, and for the first time, an uncomfortable little flare of uncertainty tried to find purchase in his gut. Like this was not smart, to twist your entire life to accomplish one thing.

But he'd made a promise. To himself even more than his mother.

Dante would pay. If nothing else mattered besides that simple fact, he would not worry about *after*.

CHAPTER TWELVE

SAVERINA WAS GETTING too used to lunches with Teo. *Time* with Teo. That had been all fine and dandy when she'd thought this was real, but no amount of knowing he saw this as little more than a business deal could stop her heart from aching for more.

Case in point, the leap her heart had taken when she'd looked up and seen Teo there early. It was just impossible to get over someone when you shared so much time together, no matter how much you understood it could go nowhere.

Harder still when, the further they got into their plans of revenge, the less she could blame Teo for how he'd gone about things. It was so easy to see he had used his plans for revenge as a replacement for grief. That he had not considered *her* feelings, because he was so deeply in denial about his own.

She worried for him now—when he got his revenge, what would be on the other side of it? Would he simply find something else to focus on while his denial grew stronger, or would he finally have to experience all those feelings he was trying to stave off? Both options seemed a terrible thing to deal with alone, and he was so very alone without her.

He is not your responsibility.

She walked next to him on the sidewalk to their regular restaurant and wondered what it said about her that she could not get that through to her soft, vulnerable heart.

They were seated as they almost always were in a little corner of the patio, with the exception of when the weather was bad. Today was bright and sunshiny, and it was nice to get out of the office and enjoy the breeze and people-watching.

They didn't only speak of Dante at their lunches. Sometimes they were seated too close to others to get deep into their plans. Sometimes there was just nothing else to say.

And sometimes, she tried to engage him in conversation about his mother, because she couldn't just let it go no matter how she knew she should. If he actually *dealt* with that grief…she wouldn't let herself *count* on things being different, but she didn't see the harm in acknowledging it was *possible*.

Maybe Teo didn't love her. Maybe he never would. But he certainly *liked* her well enough.

Today he seemed…distracted. Grumpy. She almost laughed to herself at how little he'd enjoy that description. It didn't matter, though. She had a very specific topic of conversation to go over with him today regardless of his mood. "I spoke to Lorenzo and Brianna last night."

He'd been looking off into the distance. Brooding. Now his eyes were sharp and on her. "And?"

"I told them we'd started seeing each other. That we had been for a while, but it was getting serious, so we had decided to tell people. They'd already heard some rumblings after the gala, so they weren't exactly surprised."

"Were they approving?"

She hesitated. Even now, she wasn't sure *what* their reaction had been. She'd expected a little bit of…something. She wouldn't have been surprised if Lorenzo had even thrown a tantrum about her being too young, or that Teo working at the same company was out of the question, or *something*.

But they'd been very…distant about the whole thing, which was not like *either* of them. "They were not *disapproving*."

Teo raised an eyebrow. "Is this something we should be concerned about?"

"No, I don't think so. I've never told them about anyone I've dated before. I suppose they weren't quite sure what to do with it." Which was true enough. She'd understand better once they were back home and she could gauge their expressions. The phone conversation had just felt…careful, when Lorenzo and Brianna were never careful with her.

"What would your mother think of all this?" she asked. It was not the most subtle of topic changes, but it was the only way she knew how to deal with the *yearning* inside of her. Maybe if she pushed him too far, he'd break, and she could go back to her solitude. She could have the space to get over him.

And maybe…

She could not let herself finish that thought. She could not dream of happy endings. She would not allow herself delusions. Only practicality and self-awareness would get her through this, happy or at least accepting of whatever outcome occurred.

His frown deepened, and he looked off into the distance again. "I cannot fathom."

But based on his expression, she thought maybe he was fathoming right now.

"Would she approve of the revenge plot?" Saverina continued, posing it like a general question as she focused on taking a bite of her pasta.

"No," he said quickly. "She…she was too soft-hearted to want such a thing. I think she had told me his name in hopes I'd let it go. Or perhaps to ease her conscience. It was not for revenge. That was not in her."

"But you won't let it go, even though she might have wanted it?"

He fixed her with a sharp gaze. "I will not. I am my own man. I do this in her honor, because it is what is right. Not because it is what she'd want. She isn't here."

Saverina pretended to contemplate this. "Do you believe that? Death is the end?"

"What else would it be?"

Saverina shrugged. "I took a philosophy and religions class at university. There are all sorts of theories on what happens after."

"Theories. Because there are no facts except bodies in the ground. Now, we need to talk about the museum opening Saturday. If you've told Lorenzo we are dating, there's no point to pretending these things anymore. We will arrive together, stay by each other's sides, and leave together. Everyone will know we are together, no questions."

He was very good at that. Giving her just enough leeway in a conversation to think she was getting somewhere, and then shutting her down. She studied his face in the dappled sunlight. She'd always *let* him shut it down. With everyone else in her life, she was quite happy to poke and poke and poke until she got what she wanted.

But she'd always been just a shade afraid to do it with Teo. He sent out warnings, and she heeded them. Because, in that heady beginning, she'd been afraid he wouldn't love her. She hadn't realized it at the time, but realizing it now was embarrassing. She'd always prided herself on being so strong, so blunt and fearless with people.

She hadn't been those things with him in the beginning. She'd been more like her mother, who she'd vowed to never be like. She couldn't keep going down that road, because this was no longer the beginning. Saverina was no longer under the illusion it was real.

So she needed to be herself. To keep poking at him. Especially since a little flutter of panic wriggled

in her stomach at the thought he might end this—
when she should relish the thought. No more backing
off. No more being afraid. It was time for her to…
listen to her own mind, and her own heart. No matter the consequences.

She carefully twisted pasta onto her fork, lifted
it. Steeled her spine and mustered some courage that
had sorely been lacking on her end in this relationship. "Why are you so afraid to discuss it?" she asked
him before popping the pasta in her mouth.

His affront was truly a thing of beauty. The way
he straightened. The way his expression grew very
cold and he seemed to somehow grow taller. No wonder he'd been so successful at Parisi. He knew how
to wield his expression like sharp, deadly weapon.

But since she'd been attempting to get a reaction
from him, the weapon caused no damage.

She smiled instead of wilting.

"I cannot fathom why you would consider my rational disinterest in *philosophy*, of all pointless, ir-
relevant topics, *fear*, but I assure you, it is not fear
that causes me to have no patience for such banal
conversations."

"Then what is it?" Saverina asked, imbuing her
voice with as much innocence as she could muster.

"Pointlessness. Waste of time. I abhor both."

She pretended to think this over. "That's funny.
All these lunches and evening events feel like a waste
of time to me. People are whispering about us. My
family knows. Dante no doubt knows after the gala
that you are cavorting with his sworn enemy's sis-

ter. Yet here we are, still dancing about. If I didn't know you so well, I might think you actually liked spending time with me."

She wasn't fishing. A few days ago, that's what a question like that would have been, but now… Something had changed the other night. She'd been so vulnerable in front of him. Her panic attack. Explaining why she didn't want to work in the IT department. He was the only man she'd ever shared her body with. He knew more about her than just about anyone. She had opened herself to him.

She would let him go when this was all over. She was *determined* to let him go if that's what he demanded. She would not beg. She would not twist herself into her mother.

But what she would do in this time between now and then was demand more of him. Without fear. As they worked toward that end, she would work toward… answers. Simplifying the complicated things that lay between them.

The truth was, everything between them was complicated. By his lies, his issues, and her own insecurities. She knew he'd put up with her for his revenge even if he didn't like her at all, but she wasn't sure he was quite as good an actor as he thought he was. Because if she looked back on their relationship now, she could tell how different things were in the beginning.

She'd chalked it up to her own nerves, the awkwardness of the beginning of a relationship, but he'd been playing her. Using fake charm and smooth lines. He'd been gauging her every response, then adjusting for it. He'd swept her up and away, yes, but she couldn't help but think he'd been a little swept away too.

Something had happened that first time they'd kissed, then again when he'd taken her to bed for the first time. Everything had gotten messier. Less calculated. Sometimes he'd said the wrong thing, or they'd bickered. Sometimes his temper had flared— and he'd tried to hide it, but couldn't fully.

She couldn't say he'd gotten *careless*, but he'd gotten less *aware* that every moment they spent together was his own fiction.

She knew in his head he simply saw these things as attraction. Probably luck of the draw he'd chosen someone for his revenge who suited him well enough. He did not see it as real or love or anything she couldn't seem to let go, but that did not mean some reality and some love weren't *there*.

Saverina would not let herself *hope* for him realizing that. She would not sacrifice herself at the altar of *maybe he will love me someday.* But what she *would* do was acknowledge the chance that Teo cared for her more than he was willing to admit to himself.

"I *did* like spending time with you. Once," Teo said pointedly.

She realized how that might have hit her like a blow just a few days ago. Certainly a few weeks ago, when she'd believed in his unspoken love, that comment would have hurt.

Today she stayed relaxed, even smiled at him as

she clucked her tongue. "Come, Teo. Doesn't it get a bit exhausting lying to yourself? Pretending you do all this to honor your mother's memory when it's only your own ego you're trying to salvage?"

It was a low blow. She knew it, but she was beginning to think that was the only way she ever got through his impeccable control. The only way to find out what truly lay in his heart. Low blows had gotten her through life, through to her brother when he'd been particularly stupid about Brianna.

Teo shoved back from the table, his chair scraping against the ground loud enough to have a few people looking their way. Which she supposed was the only reason he didn't stand.

She leaned across the table and spoke very quietly. "I'm not sure getting up and storming out in a childish temper tantrum are the optics you're hoping to achieve," she said, keeping her voice low, her expression calm. Fiery temper leaped in his eyes, but he did not get to his feet.

Triumph washed through her.

"I am not certain what you are trying to do with this new little attitude, Saverina, but it changes nothing."

Saverina nodded. "Yes, I agree. I suppose that's why I'm doing it. If nothing changes, I might as well be myself. I might as well *enjoy* myself, and watching you dance around your inevitable existential crisis is entertaining enough to try to push you over the edge."

* * *

Anger was like hot, fiery lava in his veins. Anger. Fury. Rage. Certainly not hurt. Teo would not account for *hurt* when the opinion of a billionaire's pampered little sister mattered to him not at all.

She was fooling herself into believing he might have feelings for her. Using obnoxious tactics fit for a *child* to get a rise out of him.

He would not allow it. But as he tried to even out his breathing, unclench his hand from the arm of the chair, he found the usually simple task of calming himself down difficult.

Existential crisis? Ridiculous! This was the purview of pampered, feckless fools. His revenge being about *ego*, after what that man had done to his mother? An insult of the highest order.

He did not need to react to every insult, though. He choked down the rest of his meal, and then they left the restaurant. He maintained his silence, but she chattered on as they walked out. He hoped it gave the illusion of a happy couple, but he wasn't sure his expression would fool anyone.

He was determined to get his temper under control on the walk back to the office building, have a foolish, *love drunk* smile on his face by the time they entered the building, but his temper only seemed to be stoked higher by the sunny day, by her cheerful, inconsequential chatter, the way everywhere he looked there seemed to be a couple holding hands, taking ridiculous selfies, *kissing*.

He wanted to destroy the image of every last one of them. Instead, he had to walk into their office building, and not snap at anyone who greeted them or spoke to them. He had to get into an elevator with her, the sweet smell of her perfume scenting the air like a drug that threatened to make him forget everything.

When the elevator stopped on her floor, she made a move to say goodbye, but he stopped her.

He got off the elevator with her. "We have something to discuss," he said under his breath. He thought of leading her to her office with a hand on her back, but something about the silky fabric of her shirt made him think of her skin under his hands, and if he touched her now...

She had her rules, but she had broken *his* rules by poking at him. She deserved a little turnabout. He would prove to her that she was not in control. She was *never* in control.

She swept into her office, and he closed her door, him still inside. She turned to face him, all challenge and some inner amused *knowing* that angered him to no end.

He did not move. For ticking minutes he stayed where he was, looked down at her, and finally watched her swallow in response. She still held on to her bravado from their lunch, but he saw wariness creep into her expression as he took a step toward her and then another.

But with that wariness was the spark of something else. She did not back away. She did not ward him off. She lifted her chin as he approached, as he crowded her. As he took her in his arms.

He said nothing. Words would not get his point across. *Words* would prove nothing. Kissing her and walking away unmoved would prove it all.

So he crashed his mouth to hers, damn all her ridiculous rules, and devoured. She did not push him away. Her hands slid up his chest, and then her arms banded around his neck. It was proving everything he wanted. She was weak for him.

But proving things and winning points seemed to dissolve as he tasted her again, as she pressed her soft body to his. It had been so long. He felt like a man in the desert, and she was the water he'd been seeking.

Her warmth, the soft give of her mouth, the way she threw herself into a kiss like nothing else could ever matter, and he got just as lost. All that coiled anger and tense frustration leaking out of him. So that the kiss was no longer weapons drawn, a gauntlet thrown, *war*.

It was peace. It was soft, swirling relief. She melted into him, and he held her as gently as he had after her panic attack. Her hands slid down his back and up again like she was offering comfort. And he found it, there in her mouth, by combing his fingers through her soft hair. She *eased* all those barbs inside of him so that he only wanted to stay here, exactly here.

Dimly, he heard the sound of his cell ringing and felt the vibrating in his pocket. He might have been content to ignore it if enjoyment had been the point of this endeavor, but he'd lost the point.

He'd *lost*.

He wrenched his mouth away from her, disgusted by the weakness he'd just discovered in himself. He had been *punishing* her, but he had *failed*.

Her eyes were dewy, her lips swollen from him, her hair mussed. She was the most beautiful thing he'd ever seen, so perfect in his arms he *ached* there in his chest. Like a heart could be fooled into believing in love after knowing how it ended.

No. He would never be fooled. He would never love. Life was nothing but a blip, and in that blip *he* was in control. Never something as useless as a heart.

"You may think you have the upper hand, *bedda*. But you want me, and it makes you *weak*. You will always be fooled by me because you want me to love you, but I do not love. I will not love. I do not know what weakness fools humans into thinking love means a damn, but it is as ephemeral as life."

Her eyes were bright, but her expression did not look devastated the way he *wanted* it to. And he still held her.

"Yet we live our lives anyway, Teo," she said softly, her arms still around his neck. "Ephemeral or not."

He removed her arms, stepped away from her. Shut it down. Iced it out. He did not look at her when he spoke, determined it was because she was *beneath* him, not because it hurt too much.

"If you mention my mother ever again, I will end this. Here and now. I will end it in the most embarrassing manner I can fathom. And I will get my revenge on Dante without you."

"But you'll have gotten your revenge on him, which means I'll still win too."

"Trust that if you do not do what I say, I will make sure you *never* win." He jerked her door open, but before he could take his leave, she spoke very softly.

"I thought you didn't care, Teo. These are very big emotions for a man so derisive of them."

He turned, faced her down this time. The anger so ripe inside of him he knew it was only that. He leaned down, got his face very close to hers so that she would understand the fury she'd unleashed. So no one out there in the hall would hear him speak to her this way. "This is strike one, Saverina. You do not want to get to strike three." And with that, he turned and left. He told himself it was a power move, but deep down…

He wondered.

CHAPTER THIRTEEN

Saverina did not see Teo for two full days. He had his assistant cancel their lunch date both days. Saverina knew she should not read into that, but she wondered if this might actually be a good thing.

If he was avoiding her, that meant he had to feel *something* for her...didn't it? Certainly her words had caused some kind of reaction that made him not want to see her despite all his many *very* important plans.

They were supposed to attend an event tonight at a museum, and she had yet to hear from Mrs. Caruso about Teo canceling it, so she decided to head down to his office and face him before she went home at the end of the day.

She whistled to herself the whole way there. She hadn't been this happy and light since the beginning of their relationship. Back then she'd been drunk on the possibility of love, and now she was drunk on the truth. On being herself.

On poking at him until he breaks.

She laughed to herself in the elevator. It was so fun watching him get all cold and remote, because

she could see it hid the fact he was *flustered*. Teo
LaRosa might hide it well, he might rage and deny
and cut down all his enemies, but when she was honest with him, when she refused to back away from
his soft spots, *she* flustered *him*.

Heady stuff.

It wasn't that she wanted to hurt him. That wasn't
the source of her joy at all. Her heart *ached* for him
half the time. But she knew, from personal experience, things often had to hurt before they could heal.

He would never be *over* the death of his mother.
You didn't simply heal grief. But Saverina wanted
him to have a healthier relationship with that grief.
And though it hurt, a painful, aching wound deep
inside, she could stand the idea of never having him
if it meant she got him to deal with that denial.

It was strange how everything inside of her had
twisted into this new kind of appreciation for their
situation. Strange how doing the most embarrassing
things she could imagine—being fooled by him, having a panic attack in front of him—had showed her
there was nothing to fear.

She could be herself in front of him. She could
even *love* him. She could not control *him*—his re-
sponses, his feelings, his denial—but she didn't need
to when she acknowledged her own.

When she allowed herself to release those fears,
and the fear of repeating her mother's mistakes, everything seemed easier. She loved Teo, yes. It was
quite possible he'd never return that feeling, and it
would hurt. It would be devastating, even. But just

like always, she would survive. She wouldn't be alone. She had her entire family to support her.

The idea of telling them the relationship had failed—or worse, that Teo had fooled her at first—had a little kernel of panic sprouting in her chest, so she set it aside. Because today was about dealing with Teo. Not about potentially looking like a failure to her family.

She smiled brightly at Mrs. Caruso, ignored the woman's usual admonitions with a pleasant wave, and waltzed right into Teo's office since the door was open.

He looked up, and she studied his expression. A flash of something—a bit like anger, but not quite that simple. Then he cooled it all off into ice.

"Saverina," he said, her name devoid of any inflection.

"Good evening, Teo," she said with all the cheerfulness she had inside her. "How are you?"

He eyed her warily, looking her up and down before turning that gaze even colder. "Can I help you with something?"

It was such a strange realization to find that exact tone of voice might have made her wilt before she'd found out about his lies. He would have pulled that out and she would have thought she did something wrong. She would have left—chin high, because she'd always had her pride—but she would have gone home and cried a little.

It seemed the truth really *did* set you free. Maybe it helped that she didn't believe his icy stares and harsh words had anything to do with *her* now. She understood the way he reacted to her was all about his own issues.

It was freeing.

"I'm on my way home, but since you're so fond of canceling our plans lately, I wanted to make sure we're still going to the museum event this evening. Together. I did not get a cancelation from Mrs. Caruso, but you've been absent the past few days. Have you been ill?"

He stared at her with cool eyes. "I have been busy."

She nodded as if she understood perfectly. "Of course." She even smiled at him and *didn't* point out that he'd never been busy for two straight days when it came to her before. "Too busy to go to the museum event? I could always go alone, but I'm afraid there *would* be talk now that our relationship is public and we haven't been engaging in our usual lunches."

"I doubt anyone pays that much attention," he said through clenched teeth.

But she kept her sunny smile in place. "I think you know they do, or you wouldn't have set this whole plan into motion in the first place. I know you're very busy, and not at all a coward, but we did say we'd be there tonight."

His expression went very nearly volcanic when she said the word *coward*. She had to bite her tongue to keep from laughing. Who knew keeping a cheerful attitude in the face of someone's fury could be so entertaining?

"If you're still planning on attending, and still wanted to approve my outfit, you should come by the house a little early. I'll have Antonina let you in."

His gaze grew skeptical. "Is that in adherence to your little rules?"

He meant it to be insulting. Too bad he failed at that. "I've been thinking about my rules. I set them up to protect myself."

"You would be smart to do so. Always."

She nodded along. "It made sense when I was heartbroken and embarrassed," she said. Then gave an insouciant shrug. "But I'm not anymore."

His eyes narrowed, temper flashing in their dark depths. It really was hard not to laugh in his face when he was so easy to rile up. When she knew he would only care about that statement if he *wanted* her to be heartbroken. Which would likely mean his heart was a little more involved than he wanted.

"Seven thirty work for you?" she asked sweetly.

A silence stretched out, his dark and vibrating with portent. Her smile never faltered. His dark-as-night act didn't faze her now, and what a gift that was.

"Very well," he agreed eventually.

She skirted his desk, watched the little war in his expression. She had the feeling he wanted to lean *away* from her—which was a victory indeed when it came to a man like him. Even if he ended up holding his ground.

She leaned down, brushed a kiss across his cheek. "See you soon." Then she walked out of his office, feeling lighter than she had in weeks.

Teo was too smart not to see this was a trap. He just couldn't quite fathom what trap Saverina was laying for him. *Yet.*

Not heartbroken anymore. What rot. If she'd gotten over it that quickly, her heart had never been involved in the first place.

Not that it mattered, because his heart did not exist and was certainly not involved and never would be. He rubbed at the odd pain in his chest as he walked up to Saverina's door.

Too much stress. Not enough sleep. Perhaps he should see a doctor. Revenge was inching closer, and it was a delicate business. That's what kept his mind going in circles at night, certainly not memories of Saverina in his apartment and the frustration of her not being there anymore. Not missing their lunches even though it had only been two days.

No. He was not so weak and childish. Wouldn't allow himself to be.

When the door opened, it was indeed the woman who'd served them drinks the other night. Teo forced himself to smile. He was in control of his face, his feelings, all of it. And if he'd had to remind himself of that more the past few days than he had in years, well, again.

Stress.

"Saverina said to send you on up to her bedroom." The woman led him down a hall and pointed at some stairs. "She's the first door on the right."

He did not trust this letting go of her rules. The soliciting his opinion on her outfit. The inviting him to her *bedroom*. Alone. He took the stairs and braced himself for some kind of…attack. But a man only fell for a trap if he didn't see it coming, and Teo saw this coming a mile away.

Whatever it was.

The first door on the right was open, and as Teo stepped over the threshold, he came up short.

The room was an explosion of color…and mess. He looked at it all in shock. She'd always been very neat at his apartment, never leaving a thing out of place. Her office at Parisi was always elegant and tidy. She herself was always well put together.

What was *this*? Clothes everywhere. Plants in every corner, hanging from the ceiling in some places. Piles and piles of notebooks, jewelry, makeup.

A door deeper in the room opened, and out she came, her hair piled on top of her head in curling spirals. She was dressed, but barefoot. When she saw him standing there, her smile bloomed.

"Oh, good, you're here. Zip me up, will you?"

She turned her back to him, the zipper of the dress gaping open. The band of her bra was a bright, vibrant pink against the demure black of the dress. His gut tightened.

He studied her back, the elegant curve of her neck

left naked by the updo of her hair. Was this some game of…seduction?

She looked over her shoulder at him. "We don't have time to waste, Teo. I still have to decide what shoes to wear. *If* you like this dress."

It wasn't anything like the red one she'd worn at the gala. This one was not meant to hit a man over the head with her raw sex appeal. No, this little black number was meant to be a demure display of all the exquisite beauty she possessed. A tease, all in all.

Particularly now that he knew she wore a bright pink bra underneath. But he was no fool. He would not fall prey to her little game. He crossed the room to her and found the zipper there at the small of her back.

He did not resist touching her. She could put on this little act, she could claim lack of heartbreak, but chemistry did not lie, and she felt it just as much—if not *more*—than he did. He skimmed his finger along her soft skin as he pulled the zipper up.

He felt the intake of breath, heard the little shudder of it as she exhaled. But when she turned to face him, she was all sunny smiles. "Thanks!" Then she did a little turn in her dress. "Approve?"

It plunged in the front, but not outrageously so. The straps were mere suggestions of fabric rather than anything substantial, and the dress's shape swept around her, outlining the perfect hourglass of her figure.

He could not seem to come up with *words*. Why should such a simple garment affect him so? Because she had set it up thusly, laid down rules, and was now breaking them on purpose. It was *all* a game.

One he had no designs on winning, because he had no desire to play.

"It's fine," he returned.

She didn't even pout. Just turned to an array of shoes spread out all along the floor. "Which shoes do you think I should wear?"

He did not know why this question enraged him, but he knew he could not let that frustration show. "Approval is not playing fashionista, *bedda*."

She shrugged as if to say, *your loss*. Then spent far too long in silence contemplating the pairs of shoes. She chose an open-toed pair that showed off the pink nails that matched her bra.

Like a *dare*.

There'd never been a question that she was a beautiful woman. He'd never had to feign attraction for her. So she could not use those wiles against him, because they weren't *weapons*. They were just her.

And he was immune. He would be *immune*.

He took his time before speaking to ensure he was as cool and detached as he was determined to be.

"I do not know what game you're playing at, Saverina, but I can assure you it is not one you will win."

She sighed. Heavily. Then crossed to him and patted his chest. Like he was a misguided *child*. "Teo, it is no *game*. What you are now dealing with is simply *me*."

"And what, pray tell, was I dealing with before?"

She seemed to consider this, moving over to a

vanity. She poked around in little bowls and boxes filled with jewelry. "Insecurity, I suppose. When I thought this was all real, I was very careful around you. I didn't change my whole personality, lie about the things I like, change who I am at my core, or anything like that, so I thought it was fine. But I was careful with the truth. Careful with how readily I showed how much I enjoyed your company. Maybe I was just taking cues from you at first, but in the end, I was so afraid you would not love me if I pushed too hard, that I simply didn't push at all." She attached one dangly earring that sparkled in the light, and then the other, as she studied herself in the mirror.

When she finally turned, her expression was one of complete control. He didn't want to believe this little speech of hers, but it was hard not to when he realized he'd never seen this expression on her face before. He'd seen what she spoke of. Always just a hint of being careful.

"I have to thank you, I think," she said. "For lying to me. It taught me a valuable lesson. Because if I'd been honest, if I hadn't been so afraid of…failing at relationships or whatever, I would have been *fully* myself, and maybe this would have gone differently. If I'd been open and honest about my feelings. Then again, maybe it wouldn't have. Maybe you have it in you to lie and manipulate someone who's in love with you, but I don't think you do."

"You'd be surprised, *bedda*." He would do *anything* for his revenge. That had always been the plan. Whatever it took. Maybe he'd lost sight of that, but she had reminded him. *This* had reminded him. He was not nice. He did not care for her feelings, her panic attacks, *her*. The foolish fiction of *love*.

All he cared about was his revenge.

"Maybe," she agreed, so damn readily he wanted to rage. "But it is of no matter. Because my lesson is learned, and now I will not fear being myself, feeling all my feelings around you. If you do not like that version of me…" She lifted an elegant shoulder. "It is your problem. Not mine."

CHAPTER FOURTEEN

SAVERINA HAD NOT fully realized how many eggshells she'd been walking on all this time with Teo. A shadow of herself. It should be embarrassing, maybe, but it was hard not to chalk it up to a learning experience. She was young. All in all, it had not been the most traumatizing first love a person could endure.

Now that she had let most of her anger go, now that she saw this whole experience as just that—an *experience*—to learn and grow from, she could sit back, relax and enjoy.

Oh, she was still in love with him. That wouldn't be easy to get over. But it was *possible*. And maybe, just maybe, she'd be able to get through to him. Show him that his grief was not the enemy, and his revenge could never assuage it.

She wouldn't shrink herself to make that happen, and *that* was the difference between real love and what her parents had done to one another.

She watched the city go by, content with Teo's brooding silence tonight. The fact he *was* brooding, *was* irritated with her, was only a good sign. Much like the realization she'd come to earlier about him lowering his guard with her after the first few weeks of wooing her with fake charm and smiles. When Teo couldn't control his anger, frustration, or whatever this was, that meant there was something deeper at play.

Poor hurting man. So determined to fight away all those feelings. Maybe they needed to get their revenge over with so he could get to that other side and *realize* he needed to deal with his grief.

She'd done some digging on Dante's wife, Julia. She'd gone back over everything she'd found when the attack had first happened and tried to coordinate a plan on what she could hack into that would give them answers. She had a lead to tug. She hadn't told Teo the work she'd done, not just because he'd been playing scarce, but because she'd wanted to get *something* for sure before she admitted to him she was trying to.

She might be growing, maturing, *evolving*, but it was a process, not an immediate cure. She'd likely always have panic attacks, so mitigating her triggers wasn't *cowardice*.

Or so her therapist had told her.

The limo joined a line of cars in front of the museum. The wealthy and elite glittered as they got out of their cars and made their way up the lighted walk to the museum.

Before the limo came to a full stop at the dropping-off point, Teo took her hand.

Every time he touched her, her heart still leaped.

She still *hoped*. But that didn't make her a fool. She wouldn't let it. She would not fall into the trap of believing love was inconsequential any more than she would allow herself to treat it like a drug.

As she'd once told Teo, it required trust and respect. She would not settle for love without it. But that didn't mean she had to abandon *all* hope she could help him, open his eyes, find the heart of him.

He took the ring he'd once given her and moved it from the pointer finger to her left ring finger. "Tonight there will be no doubt."

Her breath caught, too many things fighting for purchase in her gut. It wasn't *real*. But, oh, this ring and his serious expression made that easy to forget. "But I've *just* told my family we're dating. I can hardly—"

"The timetable has moved up." He got out of the car before she could mount an argument.

She inhaled deeply, let it out. She wouldn't scramble after him. She wouldn't be predictable. How would an emotionally mature person handle this? She got out of the car when he opened her door, took his offered hand.

When she got to her feet, she met his gaze with a bland, calm one of her own. "I don't *have* to do this, Teo."

"Then don't."

Calling each other's bluffs. But the time for bluffs was over. The time for careful and tiptoeing and *plans* was over.

He tucked her arm into his, smiled at someone

who greeted him, and pulled her forward. She went, not wanting to make a scene, but once again, she chose to see this as a good thing. Proof he was rattled.

"Why did we move up our timetable?" she asked, plastering a social smile on her face as they moved forward into the museum.

"You accused me of wasting time. Well, perhaps you were right. Perhaps I was being too careful. Now we'll move. Full steam ahead, because that is my plan, and my plan is the only one that matters."

"You seem very adamant about that. So angrily sure that it's all you could possibly want or care about."

"Almost as if I have been crystal clear about that for a while now, *bedda*." He moved them toward a man with a tray, handed her a flute of champagne. "Why not find some of your little friends who love to gossip about Parisi?" he said dismissively. "Make sure to flash that ring about."

Saverina thought about being difficult, but doing it here wouldn't suit their revenge narrative. As much as she thought Teo needed to understand there was more to life, more to *him* than this revenge, she also wanted to see Dante pay.

Especially if her theory that he'd attacked his own son turned out to be true. So for the next few hours, she would play her role. After the event, she would try to poke at Teo again.

She found a few of the biggest office gossips, started up a conversation, until they inevitably noticed her ring. Some just got wide-eyed and didn't mention it, though they'd no doubt take it back to their friends who might care about such things.

However, Nevi, one of Saverina's least favorite people at Parisi, immediately grasped her hand. "Oh, my! Look at *that*!" She looked up at Saverina, eyes all wide…but calculating. "Who?" Nevi demanded.

Saverina found that a little odd. She knew it was all over the office she and Teo were dating now. Their lunches had done that. For Nevi to act like she didn't know who Saverina might be engaged to was a bit suspicious.

"Teo, naturally," she said, tugging her hand free of Nevi's.

"Teo *LaRosa*! But…he's so handsome."

As if that meant he wouldn't be interested in Saverina? She tried not to scowl, but this was exactly why she didn't like Nevi. She was the queen of trying to make everyone else feel small. "That he is."

Nevi chewed on her bottom lip, leaned forward as if they were confidants. "Aren't you worried?"

"About what?"

"Well, we all know who your brother is. This was a bit whirlwind. Aren't you worried he's just using you to get to your brother?"

Saverina looked at the woman a full, silent minute until a faint blush began to creep into Nevi's cheeks.

"Sorry. I guess that was insensitive."

But she didn't look *sorry*. She looked embarrassed. Like Saverina was supposed to have just answered the inappropriate question, not made it awkward.

It didn't matter that Nevi was correct, in a way. Teo *was* using her to get things. And if—*when*—they broke off the engagement, this is what people would assume. She would have to live with that very public embarrassment. And likely all her siblings' pity.

She could let herself panic over that, or she could focus on the evening. What mattered was Nevi not getting a win in this little game of immature posturing.

"I guess you never really know a person's true motives," Saverina said, attempting to sound very *worldly*. And like Nevi couldn't possibly understand. "You can't read their mind or anything. But I think I know him. I understand him as well as anyone can. This isn't about Lorenzo." It wasn't even about Dante anymore. But Teo *would* hold on to the belief it was.

Until she found a way to *prove* to him that he was in a deep denial. Until she could hold up a mirror to all his hurts and *insist* he face them.

So while he played the game of revenge, while Nevi and whoever else played their middle school lunchroom games, Saverina would find a way to save the man she loved.

There was a reason Teo had wanted to come to *this* event. A reason he hadn't let Saverina in on. Which was why he'd sent her off to make certain the gossipmongers saw her ring, on *that* finger, and went to work spreading the news.

News that would be the talk of Parisi tomorrow.

Far more than the gossip should anyone notice that he was talking to Dante Marino's wife at the event.

Because Julia Marino was set to attend. He'd never met the woman, but once he'd learned of her RSVP to the event—and Dante's regrets—he'd studied up on her, made sure to look at a few pictures so he would know her when she appeared.

She was speaking with a small, slight man in a shadowy corner when he sent Saverina off to stoke gossip. Teo didn't make a beeline. He took the roundabout approach to putting himself in her orbit. He watched her the entire time, even as he greeted people he knew, or pretended to study a display. Eventually, he positioned himself in just such a way so she would *accidentally* bump into him. All it took was watching her out of the corner of his eye, then stepping back just as she started forward.

She ran right into him. "Oh, goodness. So sorry." She reached out to steady herself, and he took her by the elbow. "I didn't spill your drink, did I?"

He smiled kindly, released her arm, and held up the mostly empty glass in response. "All is well. Pardon me. I must have been distracted. Lovely display, no?" he said, pointing to the bronze sculpture from some centuries ago he'd been pretending to admire.

She just kept staring at him for a full minute before she seemed to remember herself. "Sorry. You've taken me a little off guard. You look…familiar."

"I'm sorry to say, you do not." He offered a sheepish shrug. "Perhaps I just look *like* someone you know."

She nodded. Slowly. "You have a rather striking resemblance to my sons, actually."

He made a considering noise. No wonder. They would share DNA, would they not? Did she say that knowing it was true? A stab of fury tried to take purchase, but he iced it away. "Teo LaRosa," he said, offering his hand. "Perhaps we are long-lost relatives," he said with a laugh.

She didn't even feign a smile in response. "LaRosa. I knew a woman by the name of Giuseppa LaRosa once."

Teo's eyes widened. He slapped a free hand to his chest. "My mother."

She looked him up and down, then managed what appeared to be a very forced smile. "It's been years. How is she?"

"Passed, I'm afraid."

"Ah. I am sorry. She was…" Julia trailed off, looking around the room as if to escape.

"And you are?" Teo asked.

There was another hesitation. "Julia Marino. I believe your mother once worked in my household."

Teo pretended to be confused by that. "Hmm. It's possible, I suppose. In my lifetime, she always worked cleaning large office buildings. Oh, but your husband is Dante Marino, is he not? Perhaps she cleaned his building?"

Julia's expression got more and more…closed off, Teo supposed. "You work for Parisi now," she said. Flatly. Ignoring his questions altogether.

"Yes. Oh, dear. We're a bit of your husband's rivals, aren't we?" Then he gave a little chuckle. "Ah, I suppose I should not be seen cavorting with the enemy. Or vice versa."

Her blue gaze cooled. Considerably. "I suppose not. I'm…sorry about your mother, Mr. LaRosa. Enjoy your evening." Then she turned on a heel and strode away.

Teo could not let the self-satisfied grin that wanted to spread do so. He had to keep his expression bland, maybe faintly puzzled. He turned and scanned the room, looking for Saverina. Or at least hoping that's what anyone paying attention would think he was doing.

He had planted the seeds he'd intended to with Julia. What might grow from them? So many options, but any of them would give him exactly what he sought.

When his gaze landed on Saverina, she was laughing with a man Teo knew worked in Parisi's IT department. For a blinding second, he forgot about Julia. Dante. Revenge.

All he saw was her smiling at another man. Too close together. For a strange, out-of-body moment, he imagined himself *bodily* removing said man from Saverina's orbit, but the man was already walking away from her by the time Teo could see past the immobilizing rage that pummeled him.

He breathed out, his face hot, his heartbeat a rapid, rabid thing in his chest. If he stepped back from this situation, looked at the whole thing as an outsider, he might worry that this was *jealousy*.

But of course, this was all revenge, so he had nothing to be jealous of. It was about the *image* of it all.

What he found most disconcerting about the moment was that his usual denials *felt* wrong. He couldn't fully accept that he was mad about image when the very idea of another man touching her made him want to tear down the foundations of the earth.

But he would get it under control. He would... he would find a way to undo this. To reverse these strange, unnecessary, *impossible* feelings.

Saverina made her way over to him, and he was glad he'd stayed where he was. Proud that he had stood his ground. Maybe a few wayward feelings had escaped, but he hadn't acted on them. That was all that mattered.

"I think news will be all over the office on Monday," Saverina said, sliding her arm into his, easy as you please. "I'll have to call Lorenzo when we get home and let him know the happy news." She was close now, her perfume in its normal dance with ruining him entirely as she leaned in closer. "Were you talking to Julia Marino?"

"Yes," he bit out, his gaze following the man who'd been talking to Saverina.

"Why?"

"We will discuss it later."

She frowned at that, but she didn't argue. They made the rounds. Enjoyed different displays. She made him laugh with her insightful commentary about some modern art that didn't make any earthly sense to him. Then she made him uncomfortable when she got teary over an old artifact of a child's toy displayed with bits of blanket and earthenware.

"It's kind of amazing. The things that never change, no matter how many centuries have passed, don't you think?"

"I don't think about the past."

She pursed her lips and looked up at him. "Perhaps you should, Teo."

"I do not see why. I live in the present." Case in point, the man who'd been standing far too close to Saverina was *presently* talking to someone but looking at *her* while he did so. Teo angled his body to block the man's gaze from Saverina. He pointed at the ancient artifacts. "What does any of that have to do with now?"

"You live in a present informed by their past and your own, and if you don't know what any of that has to do with now, perhaps you should consider it."

"I don't see why I'd waste my time."

She sighed heavily, clearly frustrated with him, but it was a foolish conversation. Besides, they'd done what they came to do. They could leave now. Far away from anyone's too hot gaze. Once he dropped her off, he could leave these twisted, unwelcome feelings behind. He could focus on his plan. On his revenge.

On the only thing that mattered.

When they got into the limousine, Saverina immediately turned to him. "What were you talking to Dante's wife about?"

"Nothing really. Just gauging her reaction to my name, my face. She mentioned I look like her sons."

"Oh." Saverina slumped back into the seat, pushed a palm to her heart. "Oh, how awful for her."

"I doubt it was a surprise, Saverina." He didn't want to consider Julia Marino's feelings or Saverina's response to those feelings. It was just the business of revenge. "And if Dante really attacked their son, and she knows he did, I hardly doubt my existence will change her perception of her husband."

"Maybe. Maybe she knew. Maybe she hates him. But it can't be an easy thing to know your lawful husband had a child with someone else."

He did not know why this made him think of the man she'd been talking to. But as he was not jealous, and he did not care, he pushed it away. "She is still married to him," Teo pointed out. "It cannot be that hard on her."

Saverina shook her head. "You can't begin to know what she might feel or think about it. You don't know..." She let out a long sigh. "You are a brick wall sometimes."

"Sometimes?"

She chuckled a little. "I suppose it's my own fault for constantly flinging myself at it."

"There has been a decided lack of *flinging* lately, *bedda.* Toward *me* anyway."

Her eyebrows drew together, like she didn't understand. "Have I been flinging myself elsewhere that I don't know about?" she asked, as if she genuinely had no idea.

Which infuriated him. It made him feel as though he was overreacting when, of course, he was not. He'd seen her too close to that man with his own eyes, in front of all those people who were supposed to believe she was engaged to *him*.

Something had to change. She had introduced these changes, this *being herself*, and he had not pivoted yet. He needed to sort out his response, shore up his defenses. He could not let her get to him like this.

"I would simply like you to consider the optics of cozying up with another man when we're trying to convince people *we* are engaged. I did not think it needed saying before tonight, but apparently you need some educating on how to behave like an engaged woman."

She stared at him for a full silent minute. He wanted to look away. He—inconceivably—wanted to move his body in what could only be called a *fidget*. Unacceptable.

"I don't recall cozying up to anyone. Except the odious Nevi, and I don't think she is who you mean." She kept *staring* at him, like she could see through every last brick wall she claimed he had. "The only man even remotely my age that I spoke to at that event was Carlo. Who happens to be my sister-in-law's cousin. And married. We were talking about his impending fatherhood."

"It is my experience none of these things prevent a man from wanting what he should not have."

Those words felt damning…but not toward her. Toward himself.

Again, her silence dragged out, even as the limo came to a stop outside her home. His skin felt too tight, and everything inside of him too tense, like he might simply explode. He did not understand anything that was happening inside of him.

"Were you jealous, Teo?" she asked softly. All silky promise.

He barked out a laugh, too loud in the condensed air of the limo's back seat. "I am worried about how it *seems* to those we need to convince in order to achieve my only goal." He wanted to add that he did not care who she laughed with, who she touched, but the very image had his throat closing so tight he could not force out the words.

"Ah." But she did not sound convinced, and this pounded through him like an uncontrollable fire.

She turned to him then. Her knees brushing his, those eyes flashing with something he recognized all too well. A softness he did not want from her. Ever.

"You were my first. You have been my only." She reached forward, brushed a hand over his tie, the words, the gesture sending all that fire straight to his sex. "Does that make you feel better, Teo?"

"I am quite sure I do not care one way or the other," he ground out, but something primal roared through him in direct contrast to his words. He wanted to reach out. Take. Hold. Keep.

"Would you like to come in for a drink?" she

asked, still playing with his tie. "We could discuss jealousy. Flinging. Brick walls."

He raised an eyebrow at her, not at all trusting what she was up to. Or maybe it was the roaring need inside of himself he did not trust. "You really *have* thrown the rules out the window."

"Like I said, those were about protecting myself. I think…is it really living if you're always protecting yourself? Never risking? Never feeling? I suppose you get injured constantly flinging yourself at the brick wall, but sometimes you break through. And it's worth the bumps and bruises along the way."

He did not like this analogy. For a great many reasons. "You have attached a lot of *philosophy* onto sex, Saverina."

She didn't even falter. "Sex is what you make of it, Teo. I don't mind it being a little philosophical. Not with you. So, do you want to come in?"

She wanted him to say yes, clearly. She wanted some admission of jealousy. He would not give her those things…but that did not mean he had to all-out resist. As long as it was her idea. Her choice.

Because if *she* chose it, it did not have to be about any of those things he did not want it to be about. It could just be sex. Something they were very good at together. "Are you inviting me in?"

She sighed heavily and shook her head. "Teo, I'm asking you. Is that what *you* want to do? Regardless of revenge. Would *you* like to come inside and share a drink and some time with *me*?"

Words seemed to jumble. *Regardless of revenge*

when he was only made of revenge. When nothing else could *matter*—not her, not wants, not something as foolish as jealousy. *Nothing.*

"I'd be happy to invite you in, to take you upstairs, to enjoy all this heat between us, Teo. I'd be happy to forget *all* my rules, but you'll have to come out and say it, Teo. Do you want me? Is a night together what *you* want?"

She was trying to…break down his supposed brick walls. But there was *nothing* behind his walls. Just a void. "It is of no matter to me, *bedda.*"

She nodded, then reached for the car door and opened it herself. "Then I'll see you Monday at work."

She was outside in the dark evening before he could muster a response.

He would let her go. He *should* let her go. None of the *feelings* fighting it out inside of him, painful and angry, were things he could ever let win. Could ever let control him. He couldn't control loss…so he could only ensure he won. He couldn't *want* that which would lead him astray. That which threatened all the control, all the walls he'd erected these past two years.

"You have been my only." As if that could ever matter in this world. In his *plans.* The only thing that mattered was his revenge.

But his hand was on the car door handle, and all he could think about was her. *"Do you want me?"* She'd posed it like a simple question, and maybe it should be, but it felt more like he was being cleaved in two. What he wanted. What he didn't. Somehow both the exact same thing.

Want. Want. Want.

Her.

CHAPTER FIFTEEN

SAVERINA HEARD THE car door slam. She jumped at the surprise of it in the quiet night. She really hadn't expected him to…change his mind.

She didn't let herself turn around to look at him. She didn't let herself run for him like she wanted to. He had to choose. He had to put his wants above his plans. She had to *let* him do that.

But it was hard to keep walking. To reach out to put her key in the lock. To pretend she did not hear or feel him approach. She unlocked the door, even turned the knob, but before she could push the door open, his hand clasped over her arm.

He turned her around, and she wanted to close her eyes. The punch of him in moonlight would be too much. She had invited him in because she wanted him, but she needed him to want her too. If it had taken a little unnecessary jealousy to get there, so be it. But she needed some *give*, or she was just throwing herself at the same brick wall, hoping for different results.

That would only leave her shattered. She couldn't

allow herself delusions now. She was mature. She was strong. She could fight, but she couldn't sacrifice herself at the altar of his jealousy for *nothing*.

She needed more.

She looked into his eyes, and she was lost. His mouth crashed to hers and she welcomed it, throwing her arms around his neck, kissing him back with wild abandon just as she had in her office the other day.

He'd told her she was weak that day, and maybe she was. But if it felt like this, she would be weak. Just for a few seconds. The dark, dangerous taste of him. His hands in her hair. The way his heart pounded against hers.

Because his heart *was* involved. His *wants* existed beyond his revenge—*this* had nothing to do with Dante. How could it? But she needed to hear him say it. Admit it. Out loud. To them both.

She pulled her mouth free, pushed her hand to his chest. Her breathing was ragged, and her heart felt a bit like an open wound, but she had found herself in all this mess. She wouldn't go back now. She would not turn into someone she wasn't any longer.

She met his gaze, cloudy with desire and tinged with anger and fear.

But she would not be afraid. "Say it," she demanded. She'd set a boundary. He'd respect it or perish. Because this *wasn't* weak. This was a step toward whatever lay beyond revenge.

He'd made his decision already, she knew. That was why he was standing here. Touching her. Still she watched the war play out over his face. When he spoke, it was little more than a growl. "I want *you*."

She threw herself at him then. The desire working through her like a potent, heavy liquor, or maybe like that drug she promised herself love wouldn't be. It was wild and dangerous.

His hands slid over her skirt. Then his fingers curled under the hem of the fabric and began to lift up. Cool air swirled around her now bare legs, but the heat of him, of their kiss, kept her from fully feeling it.

She expected him to touch her, to take her here, so much like the last night they'd been together. Back at his apartment. His anger and frustration biting at his control. She wouldn't refuse—couldn't. This was him at his truest, and that was what she wanted.

But instead he lifted her, smoothed his hands up her legs, and she needed no further urging to wrap them around his waist. To let him carry her inside, arching against him with a needy whimper.

He stepped inside, some mix of a groan and growl vibrating low in his throat. She raked her hands through his hair, reveling in the strength of him, the perfect, tense muscle required of every step. She didn't care who saw, who reported what to Lorenzo. She only cared that she felt his skin on hers.

He walked straight to the staircase, one kiss bleeding into another. Teeth and tongue and his lips never leaving hers. He carried her all the way up the stairs, and there was no sense that his breath was ragged from the effort of doing so. No, that was all from what they made each other *feel*.

He kicked her bedroom door closed but didn't put her down. Though he did stop kissing her long enough to speak. "Your room is a disaster."

She laughed, incapable of controlling the breathless feeling running rampant through her. "Mostly I like things neat, but the room I sleep in I like to feel *lived* in." *Live*. Oh, how she wanted him to live. With her.

This would solve nothing. This was temporary, physical. An explosion of all that chemistry. Or maybe it was an expression of her love. He wouldn't accept *that*, not yet. But maybe it could be a chip in that brick wall. One he looked back to and realized it had been more, meant more.

Maybe he could believe she loved him, and that it would matter that she did, before it was too late. Maybe he couldn't ever get there. But she'd know she gave it her all. She'd given her love before she'd called it quits.

She gentled the kiss, her arms. She unhooked her legs and slid down his body until she was on her own two feet again. She didn't let him go, didn't break the kiss. Instead, she called on all the tenderness she'd ever possessed and put it in her kiss, her touch, even the press of her body against his.

There was a moment, so brief, when she thought she felt him simply…relax. Give in. *Lean* in. Like someone starved of touch…but in this case what he was starved of was *love*. And she had so much to give him. So much.

He withdrew. First the kiss, then his body. He went so far as to take her by the arms and set her back…just a step. But he didn't release her arms. They simply stood there, now a little space between them, winded and staring at each other.

He said nothing. Didn't move. Didn't let her go. Whatever warred within was something he was determined to be his and his alone.

She, on the other hand, was determined he share it. So, even with his hands still gripping her elbows, she reached forward. He didn't stop her. She smoothed her hands up the lapels of his jacket, and his hands dropped from her arms.

She pushed the jacket off, gave it a tug so it fell to the ground. She held his heated gaze as she slowly unbuttoned his shirt. Spread it and pushed it off just like the jacket. He was all muscle, tense and beautiful. That brick wall, but she could feel his heartbeat under her hand. Real and living.

She wanted to show him just *how* real. She got to her knees, reveled in his sharp intake of breath as she unzipped his pants. Freed him. Then held his sharp, needy gaze as she took him in her mouth.

She watched him the entire time, the intent gaze, the harsh cast of his mouth. Here because he couldn't resist. Not her, not the heat between them. Against all his plans, against all his strength of control, he'd gotten out of that car, told her what he wanted, because he wanted *her*.

He pulled her back, hand fisted in her hair. Then he simply held her there, looking down at her, both of them shaking just a little. He said nothing, made no move to allow her to finish or to do more.

"What do you want, Teo?" she asked, her voice a hoarse whisper in the quiet room, barely audible over the harsh echo of his own breath. His scowl hardened at the word *want*, so she smiled.

"I want to take that dress off of you, Saverina. I want to lay you out on that bed and taste every inch of you." The he gathered her up and did just that. With wild kisses and gentle hands.

His mouth roved over her body, stoking fires, teasing, then plundering, then teasing again. She was in some other world made only of nerve endings and a love so big it threatened to drown her where she lay. Until it did, in waving crashes of pleasure that nearly had her crying.

But she wouldn't do that. Not just yet. She rolled over him, positioned herself on top. She looked down at him. "I want *you*, Teo. All of you," she said, then took him. Slow. Deep.

Everything.

Straddled on top of him, looking down at the self-satisfied half smile on his face. That faded when she reached out, traced a lock of his hair with her finger tenderly. But before he could mount any of his many defenses, she moved against him. And she decided *this* was for her.

She didn't worry about him. What he saw. What he felt. She found her own pleasure. Until she was shaking out a release so potent her muscles felt weak and lax, and she all but collapsed on top of him.

"I missed this," she said, the emotion swamping her. He'd lied to her, she knew, but she thought in this he'd always been honest. They'd always been them, lost in what they could bring out in each other.

He merely grunted and flipped her onto her back, ranging over her like some sort of avenging soldier. But she knew it wasn't *her* or even her words that he fought. It was his internal response to them.

So she kept going as he slid inside. As he made the pleasure build again, spiral higher, and deeper. "I missed you. Even when I hated you, I missed you."

His grip on her hips tightened, but he did not stop. He pushed her over that last edge, eyes black as obsidian, the war all over his beautiful face. The orgasm crashed over her, a wave of light and sensation and release. "I love you, Teo," she murmured, pressing a kiss to his neck as he followed her over the edge.

He should have left. Teo knew this in his bones, but he had not. In the aftermath, he'd convinced himself her *"I love you"* was of no consequence. If she felt such things, if she refused to accept he did not—and never would—that was on *her*.

Then he'd fallen asleep, so quickly, so easily. He didn't wake up *once* through the night—not due to a stress dream, or the strange panic that had sometimes gripped him the past few months. He'd slept free and easy, like he hadn't in years.

It might have been worth it, he supposed. A good night's sleep would help his stress. Help him keep a clear mind as they barreled forward toward revenge. A good night's sleep would keep him sharp and in control when it came to Saverina's *I love you*.

"You have been my only."

But in the pearly light of morning, her hair spread out over her colorful floral sheets. Her even breathing, the soft silk of her skin glowing in the shaft of light that poked through the curtains. His ring on her finger sparkling in that same light. The need to touch her, to drown himself in her scent and never leave, to always be her only, was so big, so deep, so all encompassing, one thing was very clear.

He had made a mistake. She was a danger. Herself. Her love. All of it. It threatened what he wanted.

And still he didn't leave. He could only lie here and stare at her, wondering how she'd done it. How she'd somehow bewitched him into risking everything.

Maybe he hoped she'd press the issue when she woke. Maybe he hoped she'd be angry he didn't return the sentiment. Maybe he hoped…for too much.

When she blinked her eyes open, sleepy and warm, she merely smiled at him. Soft and vulnerable, when she should know better by now. She stretched and yawned and curled into him, even as he kept himself perfectly still.

"I want you to let me take you somewhere this morning," she murmured against his chest, her finger tracing some unknown pattern there above his heart.

Teo felt as though he needed to clear his throat but refused such a weakness. He waited until he knew he'd be able to speak firmly. "I only have the clothes I wore last night."

"I'll get you something more casual to wear." She slid out of bed, and for a moment he forgot all his self-admonitions, the very important need to get out of here, and only watched her beautiful, naked form cross the room, slide on a short silk robe and then move for the door.

She turned in the doorway and looked at him... almost as if she was memorizing the moment of him in her bed. Then she beamed a smile his way before disappearing into the hall.

His heart seemed to be gripped in some sort of vise. He could not find the sense, the wherewithal to get out of bed, to get dressed, and to tell her they had *work* to do. Not places to go simply because she wanted it.

"I want you, Teo. All of you." It had been about sex, he told himself. Over and over again, but he'd seen the look in her eyes and knew for her it was more. *"I love you, Teo."*

Well, he did *not* want that. Avoiding her, however, had not worked. She'd only come back stronger, if last night was any indication of what his withdrawal would do. So he would attempt a different approach.

He would follow along with this little day she had planned, and there would be no *I love you*'s. He would act like it had never been said, as if nothing had changed.

Because nothing *would* ever change. If she pressed the issue, he would make it clear it was *her* issue, not his. If she let things go as they were...well, hadn't that been his plan all along?

He would enjoy it until his revenge was set. And then, if she didn't, he would end things. But first, revenge.

Always and only revenge.

She returned with a little stack of clothes and came over to hand them to him. He took them, against all the declarations in his mind to do otherwise. He frowned at the men's clothes.

"Are these your brother's clothes?"

Saverina shrugged. "He's the only man I live with. Aside from Gio. But I'm not sure a five-year-old's clothes would fit you. Come on, now. I'd like to do this before breakfast."

"What is *this*?" he asked, but he got out of bed and dressed while she disappeared into her en suite bathroom.

"A surprise," she said firmly. She reappeared in black jeans and a pale pink sweater, her hair swept up in a band. She slid her bare feet into shoes and was out the door in under five minutes.

"I have never seen you get ready remotely that quickly."

"I doubt very much we'll be seen," she replied, leading him out of the house and toward a large garage. She opened one of the doors with a button on her key and then led him to a very, *very* small if flashy sedan.

He looked at the car dubiously. "I'm not sure such things were built for men of my size, *bedda*."

"You can push the seat all the way back. It's a short drive anyhow."

She got into the driver's side, and Teo could not fathom the last time some person who wasn't a hired driver or himself had driven him around. It felt completely abnormal getting into the passenger side. Pretzeling himself into the seat that was indeed too small even with the seat pushed back.

Almost as if she was putting him off-kilter on purpose. Well, she was going to find that he did not fall apart quite so easily. Today would be proof. To her. To himself. No amount of weak moments, no amount of pressure in his chest, no amount of her beautiful smiles would change his end game.

He was in charge. Not these feelings she was trying to pull out of him. He'd never let them win.

They drove, as she'd promised, only a short while. Not even venturing into the city limits. She turned into the gates of a cemetery. Everything inside of him turned to ice. His mother was buried here.

"Saverina." But she took a turn—away from where his mother's grave was. Drove to the opposite side of the cemetery and parked. She got out without a word. He knew better than to follow her.

He did it anyway, as though she'd created some magnetic force he couldn't escape.

She walked unerringly down a narrow path and straight up to a well-kept gravestone, shining white in the sun. A delicate angel statue stood atop it.

He read the name engraved on the stone: *Rocca Parisi*. He thought at first it was *her* mother, but the dates were surely wrong as they made this woman only thirteen or fourteen years older than Saverina.

"My sister," she explained, as if sensing his confusion. "Lorenzo did not want her buried with our parents, when they failed her so completely." She knelt next to the stone, wiped at some dirt that had accumulated, pulled at some grass that grew too tall at its base.

Teo could not find words as he stood awkwardly on the path. She had mentioned sisters before, but he did not recall the name Rocca. Of course, she had what seemed like a hundred siblings, so aside from Lorenzo and the other brother he'd met who worked at Parisi in Rome, Teo could not keep them straight. But he knew she had never once mentioned a sister who'd passed away, even when she'd mentioned her parents' deaths often.

"She and Lorenzo were the oldest. Twins. I idolized them both, but Rocca was first. I guess because she was a girl too. My other two sisters are so… sweet. So soft and gentle. Rocca was…fearless. Bold. I wanted to be like her when I was very young, but then…"

Saverina sighed, brushing her fingers across the engraved name. A tear slid down her cheek. "My father never could keep a job, so eventually that fell to my mother. She got into prostitution. When she was pregnant with me, my father forced Rocca to take my mother's role."

Teo had considered himself quite aware of the depravity of humanity, but this shocked him to his core. He knew she'd grown up poor, but the wealth of her brother in the present hid just how much they'd really struggled with.

"Years later, she died by suicide," Saverina continued. "I was twelve when it happened. Lorenzo had begun to build Parisi. He had all these plans to help her, to save her, but he couldn't save her from the pain that made it impossible for her to go on."

"Why do you tell me all this?" Teo asked, his voice rough. His heart, the heart he was trying not to admit existed, ached. An ache so deep, so painful, it reminded him of losing his mother all over again. It was...too horrible. And if he allowed himself to look back on some of the things he'd said to her about her pampered lifestyle, he might actually feel *guilt* over it.

Saverina took a deep breath. She left her hand on her sister's name and looked up at him. Tears in her eyes, on her cheeks.

"I cannot wish her life away, the love I had for her. She meant too much to me even in that short period of time. I struggled with the grief of it, the guilt of it, the *waste* of it for a very long time. The pain doesn't go away, but the struggle gets...lighter when you face it. But I cannot ignore it, wish it away, avoid the *good* that kind of love does in a life. I understand denial, Teo. I have been there. I speak easily of my parents' deaths because I didn't...they weren't good people. I don't speak of Rocca very often, because it hurts so very much."

. So this was all about…him. He should feel anger. Fury, really. But he did not recognize the emotion battering him. It wasn't as hot and sharp as anger. It was something far more complicated.

He wanted nothing to do with it. But sympathy warred with a desire to be harsh. When he spoke, he did so carefully.

"I do not know what you wish to do here, and I do not wish to argue in a cemetery, but I am not in need of a secondhand psychologist."

She nodded and got to her feet. "All right then."

And that was it. She did not push the matter. When they returned to her house, he said he had to leave. She gave him a hug and a kiss, said a dreaded *I love you*, and then let him go.

But Teo understood what she'd done, because he could not get the image of the gravestone out of his head. The pain of such a sad story, of Saverina going through all that loss, out of his heart. Of her somehow still believing love could be anything but a weapon made to hurt.

She had cursed him. Again.

And it had to be the last time.

CHAPTER SIXTEEN

SAVERINA DID NOT know what Teo's next move would be, but the silence as Saturday moved into Sunday was clear enough. He wasn't going to *deal* with her *I love you*, or the point she'd been trying to make at the cemetery telling him about Rocca.

But maybe this would be a series of steps. She had pushed him…he'd isolated, and then they'd had their night together and the moment at the cemetery.

He hadn't been unmoved. Maybe he hadn't known what to do with it all, but he'd felt *something*. That was all she was allowing herself to hope for. That was all she was *trying* to allow herself to hope for.

She video chatted with Lorenzo and family in the morning. It was awkward, she could admit. She figured they'd heard through the grapevine about the engagement, but she could not bring herself to tell them a lie. So she avoided the topic, and neither Lorenzo nor Brianna pushed.

At lunch, she received a text from Teo, which was strange. He was not much of a texter. He preferred a call or to speak through his assistant.

But the text was simple.

Dinner. My apartment. Six.

It was not a request, she noted, and a text message didn't feel particularly promising in terms of getting through to him. It whispered too much of cowardice, but the man was a bit of a coward when it came to her. She decided to take that as a compliment.

She was a danger to *him*. Which meant he had *some* feelings. It had to.

She spent the afternoon deciding what to wear. It was a bit like playing chess, she supposed. Taking him to the cemetery had been honest, genuine, but it had also been a move. An attempt to get him to capitulate to his feelings by showing him hers.

Now he would offer a countermove. Maybe he'd attempt to put some distance between them. That seemed to be his MO. So she opted for casual. Much like this morning, she would sweep in and please *herself*. Tell him the feelings she wanted to tell him, and not worry about *him*.

She pulled on some jeans and her favorite sweater because it was soft and she thought the bright, vivid blue looked good on her. Especially when she let her hair down and only did minimal makeup.

Then she drove over to his apartment at the appointed time. She gave a fleeting thought to all those rules she'd laid down to protect herself not all that long ago. It had been a natural reaction to betrayal, but now that she'd stepped back, processed those lies, she could protect herself in the *right* way.

Because there was protecting yourself so carefully, risking so very little, that there was no way of gaining anything, really. That's what she'd *been* doing, most of her life. A bit like Teo hiding away from his grief, she'd been hiding from the potential for failure.

She had to be willing for this to backfire, for it not to work out, to ever hope that it might work. She had to be willing to feel pain and embarrassment or she'd never enjoy *anything*. Life would be a bland, boring existence and she'd get walked all over.

This entire experience had opened her eyes to that.

She needed to protect herself from letting that fear win, not from the ways the world and people might disappoint her, or vice versa.

She greeted everyone in Teo's building as she made her way up to his floor. He let her in almost right away, but quickly sidestepped so she could not offer a gesture of affection.

Saverina might have laughed, but she was having trouble holding on to that, light, tickled response to all his evasions after yesterday morning. She wanted to find this humorous again, but…she was just getting tired.

"Thank you for coming," he greeted her smoothly. All business Teo.

"Of course," she replied, surveying the apartment. The dining room table was set, and something in the kitchen smelled delicious. She might have deemed it romantic, except there was a laptop open at each spot on the table. A business dinner. She tried to keep her smile in place. She could not control him, only her reaction to him.

"This is an interesting setup."

"I've followed some lines on Julia Marino. There's something I'd like you to try to get to the bottom of for me." He gestured at one of the seats. Opposite the other. The whole length of the table between them.

She studied him as he took the other seat. His expression was carefully neutral. She couldn't help but wonder if he saw this as some kind of punishment. She'd panicked about trying to look deeper into Dante and Julia's son's attack, and he hadn't pushed her…until she'd pushed him.

But in the end, she just didn't think he was that vindictive. Funny when they were dealing in revenge, but his actions regarding her always seemed to boil down to fear…not actually wanting to hurt her.

Hopefully she wasn't fooling herself.

"I can try," she said, keeping her easy smile in place as she slid into the seat across from him.

"I had someone do some preliminary research, and they found an abandoned and wiped legal document of some kind, generated by Julia Marino through a lawyer who is not on Dante's payroll. I was hoping you could potentially tug on this lead and see what you might be able to come up with."

She should not be hurt he had someone *else* do preliminary work. Like she was *incapable*. She'd been on the same stupid lead, but she hadn't told him because of all that pesky *fear*. "Was Francesca Oliveri the lawyer in question?"

His expression gave nothing away, but he paused and studied her for a moment. "You've been digging."

"I told you I would try," she said, keeping her eyes on the computer. She poked around at what kind of software it had, what capabilities. "And so I have been trying."

"You didn't say."

"No, I didn't want to until I had something concrete." She looked up at him. "I'll need a pen and a pad of paper to keep some notes. And some food. You said dinner, and I didn't eat."

"So I did." He walked into the open kitchen, lifted the lid off a pot. Saverina was distracted from the computer for a moment. "You cooked?"

"A chore I do not mind taking on now and again." He plated some pasta and vegetables, and her stomach rumbled. She looked at him in wonder for a moment as he set a plate and a glass of wine next to her elbow.

It was amazing to her, how much they had in common. They'd grown up hard—he'd no doubt learned to cook to help his mother. She had never had to because the existence of her siblings had allowed her horrible beginnings to be shaped in a new, different, safer way, while he had simply been abandoned at his mother's death. He'd only ever had the woman who'd raised him, and then no one. Except a man who refused to acknowledge him.

She wanted to reach out and hug him, but she understood that expression on his face. He'd drawn a line he would not allow her to cross tonight. He would be cold and cruel if he had to be.

She might have considered crossing it anyway, but she felt bruised. She ached for what *could* be if he only let it. She blew out a breath and returned her attention to the computer.

With a pressure-filled task at hand, she just needed to focus on that. Get the revenge over with, then deal with all *this*.

She began to work, eating the delicious pasta as she went without much thought. Digging into the lawyer was just difficult enough to keep her attention on it, rather than on Teo or the pressure to accomplish this. She had already done a lot of the legwork. The next step was a little trickier. She had gone through the lawyer's personal digital footprint, but getting past the law firm's security systems had been a challenge she'd have to work herself up for.

She was irritated enough with the way Teo had set this up, she felt just up for the challenge now. Of course he'd be *this* prepared.

She hacked into the law office's systems. Worked on dealing with encrypted files most people would never be able to get into. It took time, both getting through the systems and then wading through to find what information she needed. Teo never pushed.

Never showed any impatience. He refilled her wine and served dessert.

She barely touched either.

Eventually she found a few documents related to the abandoned case. There was a document the lawyer no doubt thought she'd deleted, but Saverina managed to salvage, that included a scanned written statement from Julia.

It was a complex legal document, but Saverina tried to pull out the pertinent facts. "The day after their son's attack was reported to police, Julia started divorce proceedings. They accuse Dante of being violent with her son, Dantino."

Teo was immediately at her side, scanning the document on her screen himself. "Why did she abandon the case? Why not destroy him then and there? Why go to a lawyer and not the police?"

"I'm guessing because Dante had already gone to the police and blamed Lorenzo the night of the attack. She knew they wouldn't believe her over him."

Saverina dug deeper, trying to find more. Reason for the proceedings to be terminated. Somewhere in writing. Then she found it. An encrypted file, hidden in old deleted ones. It was the lawyer's notes.

Client abandoned case. Assailant bought her out. Ensured safety for silence.

Saverina's heart ached for a whole new reason. That poor Julia Marino had tried to leave her husband, protect her son, but had instead made what essentially was a deal with the devil. To ensure protection for her son. What a terrible situation to be put in.

Saverina looked up at Teo. "We can't use her or this."

"Why not? It proves everything. The worst of the worst. It will ruin Dante forever."

Saverina stared at him openmouthed for a moment or two. "Did you *see* why she dropped the divorce proceedings, Teo? She's protecting herself and her child. We can't just…ignore that for a little revenge."

"I don't see why not. It is the truth. The information coming to light will have nothing to do with her, or her now adult son, so what does it matter?" He walked away from her and toward his own computer, like he was going to start making plans immediately.

He clearly wasn't *listening*, so blinded by his own plans. "You know as well as I do, Dante won't care about *who* leaked this information. He will only care that it has been leaked and hurt anyone involved. He'll blame her because he thinks she's the only one who'll know. If he's capable of hurting his own son, he'll hurt her. She's *afraid*, Teo. For herself. For her son. That's the only reason she dropped the divorce."

"I think he'll be too busy being hurt to hurt them back," Teo said, not even looking at her.

She shook her head, panic and worry moving through her. And something else. Anger. "You are such a man sometimes. With the money and power Dante has, you cannot guarantee that. Even if he gets in *some* trouble, it won't be enough to ensure they're protected. Teo, you cannot use this. We have to stick to *our* plan and leave this be."

"I disagree."

She got up, strode over, and took his laptop off the table, closing it and setting it aside. "I don't care if you disagree. I will not let you use this."

"You do not have a say. Revenge has always been the plan. He will pay for what he did. To my mother. To me. This is better payment than I could have dreamed. Why should I abandon it just because you don't like it? *You* don't matter."

He said it so…off-handedly, and it cut through her like a stab wound. *You don't matter.* No, she'd been fooling herself to think she could. Perhaps underneath all his issues he might care for her in some way, but it would never matter if he didn't face his issues.

She might have given up and walked out the door if something bigger wasn't at stake. She felt like she owed it to Julia Marino to keep fighting in this moment.

"Your mother is gone, Teo. It isn't fair. It's awful. But hurting Dante won't bring her back."

He stood, his expression nothing but ice. "I have no fantasies about bringing her back, Saverina. I watched her waste away. This is not about *her*."

But it was. Even if he didn't admit it. To her or himself. She pressed her hands to his chest so he couldn't reach for the computer. "Teo, doesn't this denial hurt? How can you bury it so deep? You lost her, baby. It's okay to grieve that, to feel that."

He removed her hands from his chest, then held

them by the wrists, glaring down at her. "Enough. I have what I need. You will go now."

She stepped back. Her heart just *ached*. She couldn't get through to him. Now that he had this slice of an even bigger revenge, he'd just shut her out. Just destroy all these lives because that was the plan.

She couldn't get through to him. "I cannot be a part of this," she said, very carefully, her mind racing for ways she could save that mother and son from this...idiocy. This tunnel vision born of denial.

He shrugged. Unbothered. "I don't need you for this."

Teo convinced himself he was completely dispassionate as he watched her expression fall. He convinced himself the worry and fear and *love* in her gaze was a fiction.

He had his revenge—better even than his plan. Proof the man hadn't just refused to acknowledge his illegitimate son but had *attacked* his legitimate one. It was a boon.

He would not let her guilt him into thinking it was anything else. He would not let her ruin this. "In fact, I no longer have any use for you at all."

He expected anger, that flash of her temper, but her expression just...fell. Like he'd stabbed her clean through. He refused to acknowledge that her expression felt like his own wound.

"I know you want to compartmentalize," she said, very carefully, like every word hurt. She even pressed her hand to her stomach like she was putting pressure on a bleeding wound. "I know you're in denial about your grief. But I know, Teo. This will not change any of that hurt or grief for you. It will not make those feelings you fight away so hard disappear. Putting innocent people in the middle of all this will only cause you more guilt. More pain. At some point there will be too much to ignore."

"I have no need for your continued pseudo psychoanalyzing, Saverina. And I no longer need this engagement. What Dante did to his son and his wife is enough if you cannot fall in line. You're overreacting to think they'll be hurt. This isn't about them."

"You don't get to compartmentalize it all like that."

"Of course I do." He pointed at her hand, because he could not do what needed to be done with her looking at him with wet, worried eyes. Talking about guilt and grief when revenge was all he'd ever wanted and it was now in his grasp. "I will need the ring back."

The look on her face... He kept his hand outstretched, but he looked at the door behind her. Not cowardice...not hurt... No, something else. Regardless, feelings didn't matter.

"I can see begging you not to do this won't work, so I'll only offer you this piece of advice," she said, her voice raspy. "When you ruin not just Dante's world, but two innocent people's, the guilt will eat you alive. You want to play hard-hearted, detached *stone*, but you are a man. And no matter how you ignore your grief, your guilt, your *heart*, it is there.

This won't just hurt me and those two innocent people. It will *destroy* you."

Good, was all he could think. Let it. He forced himself to look at her, at the tears tracking down her cheeks, because love was loss and pain, and that's all it ever would be.

She wrenched the ring off her finger, slapped it in his palm. "If you realize what a mistake you've made, I hope you'll stop yourself. If you regret breaking things off with me in the next few weeks, I hope you'll come apologize. But if you come to me after you've done this horrible thing, once I've gotten over you, I will not take you back, Teo. I will not." She frantically wiped at her cheeks, but more tears poured out of her eyes. Eventually she lifted her chin, met his gaze. "So I would think long and hard about what you want your life—that long, precious thing you have to live no matter what—to be like." Then she turned and left.

And he was glad of it. That's why he went to the table and broke every last dish and glass on it.

Glad.

CHAPTER SEVENTEEN

TEO DID NOTHING with the information that evening. He did not sleep. He did not plan. He sat at the dining room table and looked at Saverina's half-eaten dessert. He could admit, as morning dawned over the city outside his window, that he'd brooded.

He tried to convince himself that this was for the best. Saverina was free to go after the life she wanted. Love and family and hell on earth if she asked him, but she had not.

He could admit, here, he'd rather enjoyed the idea of spending the next few years together. Not because of love. No *children*, for God's sake. Just…friendship. Partnership. A comfortable and enjoyable business arrangement.

Maybe he'd liked an image of all that, but he wouldn't regret it being over. Alone was best. Especially if she'd continued poking at him about grief and feelings. He didn't need that. He was better off alone.

He would begin the leak. Meet with his press point person. Have him withdraw all the rumors about the

Parisis and focus on Dante's violent nature. There was no need for Saverina anymore. No need for proving the Parisis were good. If Dante could attack his own son, that would destroy everything.

Poetic justice.

But instead of calling his point person, he got in his car and drove to the address he had for Julia Marino. Because Saverina was wrong. Julia and her son would be *happy* if he leaked this. He would prove it to Saverina.

If he ever saw her again. Maybe he'd quit Parisi tomorrow. He had saved much and invested well. He could go anywhere. Do anything. He had no use for Parisi, for Sicily, for women who haunted and cursed in equal measure.

He would go to the Caribbean. To New Zealand. As far away from Sicily as possible.

When he arrived at the Marino estate, the gates were closed, but there was a little buzzer and intercom system, so he used it.

"Can we help you?"

"My name is Teo LaRosa. I need to speak with Mrs. Marino."

There was a long, long silence. Then the squeak of gates opening. Teo got into his car and drove up to the expansive mansion.

He stopped his car at the extravagant entrance and got out. Something beat in him like panic, but he refused to label it as such. It was simply the realization anew that his mother had struggled all her adult life when she should not have. With this wealth and extravagance, Dante could have at *least* paid her off.

But he'd threatened her, scared her, and left her with nothing.

The door opened before Teo even got up the stairs. Julia stepped out and closed her front door behind her.

"You shouldn't be here," she said as she approached. She began to walk past him, back toward where he'd come from. He found himself following as she stalked away, clutching the cardigan around her tightly.

When they got past the fountain, she finally stopped and turned to face him. Her expression was cold. "The cameras cannot see us or hear us here, but I will need to return immediately. Drive down the street to the park on the corner. I will meet you there. You haven't gone to the press yet, have you?"

He blinked once in confusion, before it dawned on him that Saverina had *warned* her. Fury leaped through him like pain and grief, but he had no chance to ask Julia any questions.

She went back the way she'd come before he could answer. Teo could only stand frozen for a moment or two. Then he began to follow her instructions.

Because he was right.

Because she was afraid of her husband.

And him exposing her secret would save her. Saverina would see she was completely and utterly wrong, and then they could—

Nothing, he reminded himself harshly. His and Saverina's partnership was over. Done. He got in his car and drove to the park. He waited far longer than he should have for Julia to finally arrive. She didn't approach him, just went and sat on a little bench overlooking a small pond.

Teo walked over and took a seat next to her.

"Have you gone to the press already?" she asked again.

Teo could not find his voice right away. Unacceptable. "No."

Julia let out a long sigh as her shoulders slumped. Relief, clearly, and it had that ugly guilt Saverina had warned him about eating away at his insides.

"What do you want, Mr. LaRosa?" Julia asked, her voice frayed by stress and something he could not begin to guess at.

"To expose your husband for what he is. A violent criminal on top of everything else."

She shook her head, then met his gaze. There were tears in her eyes, but they did not fall. "I cannot let you do this."

Teo frowned. "Why not?"

"I don't know how you found this out, but I know who you are. It's impossible to ignore the resemblance between you and my sons, the way your mother left our employ all those years ago. I... I lived in much denial back then, but I don't anymore."

"Because your husband attacked your son."

She inhaled sharply, but she nodded, her hard gaze never leaving the pond. "He was drunk. He and my son engaged in a physical fight that Dante won. It was the first and only time there'd been a physical altercation. And we handled it in a way that is best for my family." Finally she turned to face him, and her expression was pleading. "So I would appreciate your discretion, Mr. LaRosa. Please don't do this to us."

The *please* landed too hard, in a memory of his mother. Begging him for something. He didn't want that memory of her in that hospital bed. A wisp of nothing. Already gone.

"Please be happy, Teo. Please."

"There will be no discretion," Teo said harshly. "I will end him. Not only will his reputation be ruined, but he could very likely face actual charges. He will be put in jail. Whatever you fear, you will be safe from."

She laughed. Bitterly. "No, I won't. And he won't face charges because we won't press them. I understand how you feel. Why you want this. Even if I don't know the details of what Dante did to your mother, I can guess. I sympathize with your feelings, I do. But I will fight you on bringing what Dante has done to light."

He did not understand this. She should be on her knees begging for his help, thanking him profusely. "How can you not want to see him ended?"

"Because with our agreement in place, my son is happy. Free to follow the life he chooses without Dante's say, but with the help of Dante's money. This was my son's wish, and I agreed because this way there's no revenge, no chance of Dante hurting us. I can hurt him worse and better. He stays away, and we get to live free of his threats. I would do anything, sacrifice anything to keep my children happy. Even allow Dante to walk free."

Teo could only gape at her. It made no sense. How could there possibly be a way not to want to see him ended?

"You don't understand," Julia said morosely. "I don't know how to make you understand. I love my children more than I need that man to suffer. Life isn't fair. It has never been fair. We could think we're evening the playing field, make it *feel* fair to us because he loses something. But it isn't fair. *Nothing* is fair. I can let that terrible truth ruin my life, or I can do this."

"And what is this?"

"Love. My children. Myself. Focus on what we have, not what we don't. A mother only wants to see her children safe, and healthy, and *happy*. Would I enjoy seeing Dante in jail? Of course. But it wouldn't last, and he is vindictive and cruel. Trust me when I say that he lives in his own kind of jail. A life devoid of love, empathy, family. He is an empty chasm of wanting more, more, more and never getting it. It will eat him alive far better than any justice system."

It wasn't enough. It couldn't be enough. "I will ruin your husband because he ruined my mother. It is right. It is fair. This…whatever you're doing…is not."

"I only vaguely remember your mother. I don't know you at all. But your devotion to her makes me think you loved each other very much."

He thought back to the day he'd said something to Saverina about everyone loving their mother. Her response about not being sure she did. He had an evil father, so he supposed evil mothers existed, but it struck him as sadder, somehow. But this was not about Saverina. "She was the best person I'll ever know."

"I am glad of it. Let me tell you, as a mother. If she loved you, protected you, got to see you grow into a man who would love her back, who succeeded, her life was not ruined. No matter what hardships she faced. And if you are happy in your life, you have honored her memory in the only way that would ever matter to her. That is all a good mother wants. Her child to be happy and fulfilled."

Happy.

Teo did not know what to say to this. Did not know how to reconcile the fact that... Saverina had been right. Julia did not want his revenge. Did not feel safe in it. And worse, so much worse, she somehow agreed with Lorenzo's philosophy on the whole thing. That love and happiness could be more important than justice.

"Will you ruin my son's life to make yourself feel better?" Julia asked, her eyes full of tears. Like Saverina's had been last night. When she'd begged him not to move forward. When she'd warned him that just this would happen.

When she was somehow right, and he couldn't find purchase in this moment. He wanted to ruin *Dante*, not these people, but...

"Mr. LaRosa? Teo..."

But he got to his feet. And left without answering

her question. Because he did not have an answer. He had nothing now. Only more and more confusion.

So much so that when he drove past the cemetery he'd visited with Saverina only yesterday, he turned in, just as she had. But he drove to his mother's gravesite.

His breath was coming too shallow, his heart beating with painful thuds against his chest. It reminded him of Saverina's panic attack. And worse, made him wish she was here, when that was over.

Over. He had no need for love. It only ended here. Here.

He did not want to do this, and yet some force compelled him. He parked and walked to her grave even as clouds slid over the sun, as thunder rolled in the distance.

Because he didn't know what to do, and when she'd been alive, he'd always known. Always been so sure.

She'd made it clear she wanted simple for her memorial because she'd known she was dying for some time before it had actually happened. Here, he'd given her exactly what she'd wanted.

Simple or elaborate, it didn't seem to matter. She was gone, and her name was etched in stone that would eventually sink into the ground and disappear.

He knelt next to the stone as if someone had pushed him into the position. He could hardly breathe. Everything inside of him was twisted into painful knots. He didn't know what to do except follow Saverina's example from yesterday. He brushed dirt off the stone, picked a few weeds out of the grass.

Rain began to fall, the day turning quickly gray. No sun. No rainbows. Just cold and wet and discomfort and his mother's name etched in stone. Gone. Gone forever. Nothing to be done about it.

So why was he here? "I do not know. I cannot fathom. I know you did not wish me to get my revenge, but I need it. I...need..."

She had loved him. She had wanted the best for him. Had begged him to be happy as she'd slipped away. Julia claimed this meant her life had not been ruined, but how could that *be*?

"Can't you show me what to do? Can't you...lead me in some way? I don't believe in this. Dead is dead, but I need... I need..."

He needed revenge, but the only thing he seemed to be able to really feel was how much he needed Saverina. She would know what to do, to say, to feel. She would know and...

She had once asked him what his mother would think of his revenge. She would not want it. Not for herself and not for him. She'd wanted him to live a life free of that. Live the life that would make him happy.

She'd said that on her last day too. Not just Dante's identity as his father, but messages of love. Of hope.

Teo, my love, you must promise me to live a good life. A happy life. And he had promised. But he hadn't known what good was. What happy could be. He'd thought it was revenge, but the closest he'd ever come was Saverina. Because plans of revenge had never made him feel *good* or happy. They had only given him a goal. A goal that would one day be over.

And then what?

Without Saverina, that question felt like a prison sentence. Which was not what his mother had wanted for him.

"You would approve of her. I am not so sure you would approve of me."

A boom of thunder shook the ground, followed by the sizzling crackle and flash of lightning. The storm was angry, but his mother had never been. It was no sign from the universe, from the great beyond. It was only weather.

"I do not know how to be happy without you. I didn't want to be." Or he hadn't. Until Saverina had upended everything. She had snuck under his defenses, made him happy against his will. Surprised him with how…nice life could be with someone like her by his side.

And when he was not happy, when he had been hurt with grief and fear, Saverina had put a gentle hand on him. She had *loved* him.

Loved him.

Rain soaked into his clothes, made the ground muddy beneath his knees. Cold permeated his skin until he was shaking.

He did not want to hurt Julia or her son. He did not want to hurt Saverina. He did not want to hurt anyone. Not even Dante, at the heart of it. Because all he'd been searching for was a way to feel better. A way to feel whole. He'd convinced himself it was on the other side of revenge, but Saverina said it wouldn't be.

She'd been right about so many things now. How could he deny she might be right about this?

He tilted his head back, let the rain pour over him. And he made a new promise to his mother.

I will try.

CHAPTER EIGHTEEN

Saverina let herself wallow most of the day Sunday. Her first romantic heartbreak called for a little wallowing, she thought. She looked at her now bare finger and felt the loss all over again.

She let herself cry. She let herself eat far too many cakes. She took a long bath, where she cried all over again. She kept waiting for it to feel *cathartic*, but mostly she just felt wrung out and awful.

She was headed for the kitchen for more cake when she heard…commotion deeper in the other wing. Like… Her heart skipped a beat. She rushed through her wing of the house to the main part, and there they were. Her favorite people.

Helena was having a little toddler tantrum. Gio was covering his ears while Lorenzo held Helena and tried to calm her down. Brianna rubbed her ever rounding belly looking sun-kissed and exhausted. They all looked a little damp.

"You're back."

"Aunt Sav!" Gio ran full throttle at her, so she had no choice but to catch him. Bury her nose in his hair.

Hold on for dear life. "You're getting far too big for me to toss in the air." She gave him a tight squeeze, tears threatening. Oh, she'd missed them. Missed this. And…she could be okay. She *would* be okay. Even without Teo, because she had them.

While Teo has no one.

Gio wriggled in her grasp until she had to put him down. Helena, distracted from her tantrum, toddled over to Saverina and demanded the same treatment as her brother. "Up! Sav!"

So Saverina did the same thing. Lifted her niece, snuggled and squeezed until the girl squealed and demanded to be put down.

Usually they made her feel so happy and light. That Lorenzo could have this, when he absolutely deserved it and was an amazing father. But today, she couldn't help feeling bruised. Wistful.

Like children were never going to be hers, when that was silly because she was so young yet. Had so much life to live. She'd meet other men. She'd fall in love again.

It felt impossible in the moment, but she had to shake away these dire thoughts and smile at her brother and sister-in-law.

Lorenzo looked her up and down, frowning as if he could see everything in her expression.

"We decided to come home a little early. Saverina—"

Before he could finish, Saverina crossed the room, flung her arms around her brother, and burst into tears. She had never done such a thing in all her life, always trying to be strong for him. But today…she only wanted to be held and told it would be okay. It would get easier to feel this horrible ache in her chest.

He hugged her close. "Do I need to kill him?" he asked in her ear.

"Yes," she said emphatically into his chest.

"Can it wait until tomorrow? I'm a bit tired from the trip."

It made her laugh, which she figured was the point. "I suppose."

"Come on, Gio," Brianna said, taking her son's hand as she carried her daughter. "Let's let Papa and Auntie Sav catch up."

"But why is Aunt Sav crying?"

"Well, I imagine the answer to that question is *men*," Brianna said with some humor as she tried to drag Gio out of the room.

"But I'm a men," Gio insisted.

"Hopefully a better one," Brianna muttered, and then they were gone.

Saverina looked up at her big brother and sighed. "I suppose you'd like the whole story."

"I do not think I will *like* it, no, but let's hear it."

She explained it all to him. Even the part about Teo tricking her. She laid it all out. The embarrassing parts and the way she'd learned, matured, grown. It made her proud of herself, actually, the way she'd crawled out of that terrible realization into a person she liked better.

"He is so focused on this revenge. But you were

right, I hate to admit. When you have love and family and real joy, the revenge no longer feels quite so important."

Lorenzo nodded. "It is a strange lesson to learn, but yes. It is true. However, this is not a lesson you can teach him. He has to accept it on his own terms, in his own time."

"I know. I *do* know that. I can even accept it if he never does. It's just… I know he loves me, but he's… he lost his mother, and he's so mired in that grief he won't deal with. If he would, if he *could*, we could both be happy. Now."

"Well. I suppose men do that kind of thing."

She gave him a sharp look, because he'd done something very similar when it had come to Brianna. His issues had been compounded by being in charge of all of his siblings for so long, for the guilt he felt over Rocca's death, but it was similar.

"I told him that if he didn't go through with this, if he apologized in the next few weeks, I'd forgive him because I love him, but if I got over him before that happened, it was over for good, and he would be sorry."

"And so he shall. Do you want me to fire him?"

Saverina blinked at her brother. It wasn't a joke like killing him. He was dead serious. "Is he good at his job?"

"Naturally. He wouldn't be in the position he is if he wasn't."

"Then it would be highly unethical of you to fire him."

"I'll be as unethical as I please for my baby sister. Hence the offer for murder as well."

"Thank you, but no. I want…" Well, what she really wanted was for Teo to show up right now and confess his love for her and tell her he'd forget all about Dante and revenge. But she needed to accept that wasn't going to happen. "It's a normal thing to have your heart broken, and I want to go through normal things. So I'll be sad and pout for a while, but I *will* get over him."

"Of course you will. The offer for murder and firing stands forever, *soru*."

She moved to hug him again. To feel the solid truth of family that would stand by your side no matter what. She'd been so lucky to have him, her other brothers and sisters. She'd never had to do any of this alone. "I'm just glad you're home."

She tried very hard to lean into the glad, and not fret about Teo not having *anyone*. She had left the door open for him. She could not make him walk through that door. So she could not be the company he needed, the love he needed, until he was willing to accept it.

"Come, I am hungry. Let us go have some cake," Lorenzo said, giving her shoulders a squeeze. Because he knew cake was her favorite accessory to go with sadness.

But before they could get to the kitchen, Brianna was hurrying up the hall.

"There's a very…wet, angry man at the door demanding to see Saverina," Brianna said with some concern. "Should Lorenzo send him away?"

"Yes," Lorenzo said in a low growl.

"No," Saverina said, slapping a hand to her brother's chest so he didn't march toward the door.

Teo was here. He was… It had to mean something good. It *had* to. "I will handle this myself. If I need help disposing of a body, I shall ask for it."

Lorenzo grunted. "Very well."

Trying to keep her gait casual, slow, Saverina walked down the hall toward the entryway. When she arrived, Teo stood there. Dripping.

He was soaked through, hair plastered to his face, muddy splotches on the knees of his expensive pants. She had never seen him in such a state. And even though his expression was dark and serious, her heart soared.

"I went to your entrance, but Antonina said you were over here with your family. Good evening, Mr. Parisi. Mrs. Parisi."

Saverina frowned and glanced over her shoulder. Lorenzo stood behind her, scowling. Brianna looked more curious than angry. But when Saverina gave her a pleading look, Brianna tugged on Lorenzo's arm. "Come. We have much unpacking to do, and I am not feeling well enough to do it."

Lorenzo's scowl did not leave his face, but he looked from Teo to Saverina.

"Please," she mouthed.

He grunted again, then turned on a heel and disappeared with Brianna. Saverina turned back to Teo.

"Is he going to kill me?" Teo asked calmly.

Saverina pretended to consider the question, then shrugged. "Probably."

"Pity. I was just figuring out how to live."

She looked up at his face, her heart fluttering against all better judgment. "Were you?" she whispered.

He crossed to her and reached out, touched her cheek with a gentleness he'd rarely shown. Certainly not while looking into her eyes like this.

"I went to see Julia. Dante's wife. To warn her what was about to happen." He shook his head. "No, that isn't true. I wanted to prove you wrong. To get her blessing and rub it in your face."

"How mature," she murmured. "But I'd already warned her."

He sighed. "Yes. So she just kept going on and on about how much she loved her son, how that mattered more to her than Dante's feelings on anything. She said…a mother only wants a happy son, and I… I know it is what my mother wanted." He bowed his head. "I did not want to think of it, deal with it. I would have set it aside forever, but between the two of you, I felt…cursed. Haunted."

Saverina couldn't stop herself from frowning, because it sounded rather accusatory, all in all.

But he continued. "I went to the cemetery. I did what you did with your sister's grave. Tidied up a bit. But I did not feel her there. Even when it began to storm. I tried to speak to her, but it was…fruitless."

She swallowed at the lump in her throat. This was

why he was wet and muddy. He'd been to the cemetery. "I do not often feel Rocca there either."

"You do not?"

He seemed to need the reassurance, and maybe she was a fool to give it. But she could not deny him this. "Not in the cemetery usually. I think... I think cemeteries are more for the living than the dead. I feel her in other ways. I'll see something that reminds me of her, and it is as if she's there with me. Looking at it too."

He studied her for a long time, his gaze raking over her face. Then his other wet hand came up to cover her other cheek.

"Do you remember the first time I kissed you?"

"I'm not sure where you're going with this, but yes." His clothes and hair were dripping on her, but she did not dare move away from his gentle grasp. "We were leaving the theater, about to go our separate ways. I wasn't sure what to make of you. You hadn't even tried to hold my hand. Then you kissed me."

"You'd told some joke that reminded me of my mother. It would have made her laugh, and my mind drifted to what it would be like for the two of you to meet. I suppose... I felt her there. I did not like it. It made me angry."

"So you kissed me?"

"I thought that would take the anger away." He shrugged. "It did. After a fashion."

"I do not think this is the grovel you think it is."

"But it is. I do not get angry. I do not let it win.

Everything is cold and calculated so I can *win*. But you have frustrated me, and I thought I could solve it in all manner of ways, but I never did. I never could solve you."

"I am not a *problem*, Teo."

And then he did something…unfathomable. He laughed. A true laugh that crinkled his eyes and made his entire being seem…lighter. "You are. But problems are not always bad. Sometimes they are something you learn from. Something that changes the course of your life. You have changed mine, Saverina. I cannot let my anger go, but for Julia's love of her sons, for my love of you, I can let this revenge go."

Her heart tripped over itself. "All of it?"

He nodded. "I think I understand what Lorenzo meant. I could hurt Dante, but it would not teach him any lessons. He is an evil man who would hurt his own legitimate son. Why should me hurting him change anything for him? It will only make him a worse person, likely. But one thing that will never make sense to him is me just…living a good life."

"What life do you want?"

He released her face, reached into his pocket and pulled out the ring he'd given her. His proposal had been fake then.

It wasn't now.

"A life with you, Saverina. I love you. It is not easy for me. I cannot promise that it ever will be. Love feels dangerous, so tenuous. Grief is the other side of love, and it threatened to swallow me whole."

She nodded and had to work hard to speak past that lump in her throat. "I'd rather live a life with grief than without all the love that is the other side of it. Grief is bearable when you share it. When you accept it. When you grow from it."

Teo inhaled deeply. "You have taught me this. By being you. By speaking of your own grief. By never being afraid to ask me about my mother, my grief. You have forced me to face that which I did not want to, but needed to. And while you did all that, you loved me. You asked me what I wanted. I was so afraid of what I wanted, Saverina, but I am not a coward. Not anymore."

He took her hand in his. "I want you. A life with you. A family with you. Will you love me? Marry me? Share your life and grief with me?"

Saverina let out a shaky breath but did not answer right away. She loved him, yes, but she had to make a decision that was best for both of them. She looked into his eyes, though, and saw truth. Because love was bright and wonderful and happy, but it came with harder things.

He'd made his peace with that. Finally. She could see it in his eyes. "Yes, I will."

He slid the ring onto her finger, and then she flung herself at him. He was cold and wet, and a mess. But he was hers.

Always.

EPILOGUE

THEY NAMED THEIR daughter after the two people they'd loved and lost too young. Every day, Giuseppa Rocca LaRosa brought her parents a joy that eased the grief that never fully went away.

When their son was born, they named him after the man who'd first showed them that revenge did not really matter when you had a life worth living. Renzo LaRosa was a terror, from the moment he was born kicking and wailing.

"He will either save the world or end it," his uncle Lorenzo had said on his fifth birthday. A bit darkly, but with the kind of love a family bonded by grief and joy understands is the most important thing.

Teo had needed some time to fully sink into that, believe in it, allow himself to express that same kind of love, but with every passing year it got easier. As his daughter grew into a charming young woman, so like her mother. As his son turned into a man who would indeed save whatever worlds he chose.

As his wife never left his side, no matter what they gained, or lost, or fought over.

As he built a relationship with his two half brothers and their mother, so that even they became something like family. As he reached out to the family his mother had hidden from for their own good, and gave them the gift of answers.

Every Parisi gathering grew larger, louder and more boisterous as the years went on. Until it was the loudness and the love overflowing in every room that became Teo's normal, rather than the small, quiet love of his childhood.

Teo appreciated them both. Grieved what he'd lost, and loved what he had in every moment with everything he was.

He rarely thought of his biological father, even when he was with his brothers, and felt only an odd, distant kind of satisfaction when Dante got himself into enough trouble with embezzling business funds to lose his business and spend some time in jail.

But mostly, he did not care what the man did. He only cared that, year in and year out, he had finally kept the promise to his mother he'd made as she'd died.

He lived a good life. A happy life. With more love than any one man surely deserved.

* * * * *

#4177 CINDERELLA'S ONE-NIGHT BABY
by Michelle Smart

A glamorous evening at the palace with Spanish tycoon Andrés? Irresistible! Even if Gabrielle knows this one encounter is all the guarded Spaniard will allow himself. Yet, when the chemistry simmering between them erupts into mind-blowing passion, the nine-month consequence will tie her and Andrés together forever...

#4178 HIDDEN HEIR WITH HIS HOUSEKEEPER
A Diamond in the Rough
by Heidi Rice

Self-made billionaire Mason Foxx would never forget the sizzling encounter he had with society princess Bea Medford. But his empire comes first, always. Until months later, he gets the ultimate shock: Bea isn't just the housekeeper at the hotel he's staying at—she's also carrying his child!

#4179 THE SICILIAN'S DEAL FOR "I DO"
Brooding Billionaire Brothers
by Clare Connelly

Marriage offered Mia Marini distance from her oppressive family, so Luca Cavallaro's desertion of their convenient wedding devastated her, especially after their mind-blowing kiss! Then Luca returns with a scandalous proposition: risk it all for a no-strings week together...and claim the wedding night they never had!

#4180 PREGNANCY CLAUSE IN THEIR PAPER MARRIAGE
by Kate Hewitt

Honoring the strict rules of his on-paper marriage, Christos Diakis has fought hard to ignore the electricity simmering between him and his wife, Lana. Her request that they have a baby rocks the very foundations of their union. And Christos has neither the power—nor wish—to decline...

#4181 THE FORBIDDEN BRIDE HE STOLE
by Millie Adams

Hannah will do *anything* to avoid the magnetic pull of her guardian, Apollo, including marry another. Then Apollo shockingly steals her from the altar, and a dangerous flame is ignited. Hannah must decide—is their passion a firestorm she can survive unscathed, or will it burn everything down?

#4182 AWAKENED IN HER ENEMY'S PALAZZO
by Kim Lawrence

Grace Stewart never expected to inherit a palazzo from her beloved late employer. Or that his ruthless tech mogul son, Theo Ranieri, would move in until she agrees to sell! Sleeping under the same roof fuels their agonizing attraction. There's just one place their standoff can end—in Theo's bed!

#4183 THE KING SHE SHOULDN'T CRAVE
by Lela May Wight

Promoted from spare to heir after tragedy struck, Angelo can't be distracted from his duty. Being married to the woman he has always craved—his brother's intended queen—has him on the precipice of self-destruction. The last thing he needs is for Natalia to recognize their dangerous attraction. If she does, there's nothing to stop it from becoming all-consuming...

#4184 UNTOUCHED UNTIL THE GREEK'S RETURN
by Susan Stephens

Innocent Rosy Bloom came to Greece looking for peace. But there's nothing peaceful about the storm of desire tycoon Xander Tsakis unleashes in her upon his return to his island home! Anything they share would be temporary, but Xander's dangerously thrilling proximity has cautious Rosy abandoning all reason!

YOU CAN FIND MORE INFORMATION ON UPCOMING HARLEQUIN TITLES, FREE EXCERPTS AND MORE AT HARLEQUIN.COM.

HPCNMRB0124

Get 3 FREE REWARDS!

We'll send you 2 FREE Books **plus** a FREE Mystery Gift.

FREE Value Over **$20**

Both the **Harlequin® Desire** and **Harlequin Presents®** series feature compelling novels filled with passion, sensuality and intriguing scandals.

YES! Please send me 2 FREE novels from the Harlequin Desire or Harlequin Presents series and my FREE gift (gift is worth about $10 retail). After receiving them, if I don't wish to receive any more books, I can return the shipping statement marked "cancel." If I don't cancel, I will receive 6 brand-new Harlequin Presents Larger-Print books every month and be billed just $6.30 each in the U.S. or $6.49 each in Canada, a savings of at least 10% off the cover price, or 3 Harlequin Desire books (2-in-1 story editions) every month and be billed just $7.83 each in the U.S. or $8.43 each in Canada, a savings of at least 12% off the cover price. It's quite a bargain! Shipping and handling is just 50¢ per book in the U.S. and $1.25 per book in Canada.* I understand that accepting the 2 free books and gift places me under no obligation to buy anything. I can always return a shipment and cancel at any time by calling the number below. The free books and gift are mine to keep no matter what I decide.

Choose one:
☐ **Harlequin Desire**
(225/326 BPA GRNA)

☐ **Harlequin Presents Larger-Print**
(176/376 BPA GRNA)

☐ **Or Try Both!**
(225/326 & 176/376 BPA GRQP)

Name (please print)

Address   Apt. #

City   State/Province   Zip/Postal Code

Email: Please check this box ☐ if you would like to receive newsletters and promotional emails from Harlequin Enterprises ULC and its affiliates. You can unsubscribe anytime.

Mail to the Harlequin Reader Service:
IN U.S.A.: P.O. Box 1341, Buffalo, NY 14240-8531
IN CANADA: P.O. Box 603, Fort Erie, Ontario L2A 5X3

Want to try 2 free books from another series? Call 1-800-873-8635 or visit www.ReaderService.com.

*Terms and prices subject to change without notice. Prices do not include sales taxes, which will be charged (if applicable) based on your state or country of residence. Canadian residents will be charged applicable taxes. Offer not valid in Quebec. This offer is limited to one order per household. Books received may not be as shown. Not valid for current subscribers to the Harlequin Presents or Harlequin Desire series. All orders subject to approval. Credit or debit balances in a customer's account(s) may be offset by any other outstanding balance owed by or to the customer. Please allow 4 to 6 weeks for delivery. Offer available while quantities last.

Your Privacy—Your information is being collected by Harlequin Enterprises ULC, operating as Harlequin Reader Service. For a complete summary of the information we collect, how we use this information and to whom it is disclosed, please visit our privacy notice located at corporate.harlequin.com/privacy-notice. From time to time we may also exchange your personal information with reputable third parties. If you wish to opt out of this sharing of your personal information, please visit readerservice.com/consumerchoice or call 1-800-873-8635. **Notice to California Residents**—Under California law, you have specific rights to control and access your data. For more information on these rights and how to exercise them, visit corporate.harlequin.com/california-privacy.

HDHP23